Ted and Emily were obviously made for each other. They even looked a little bit alike. Beth gritted her teeth when she painfully remembered how they kidded each other, made funny faces, and generally never left each other alone. She was obviously a total idiot to think that someone like Ted Sealley would go for someone who never knew what to say, who daydreamed too much, who was plain-looking and who gave everyone the feeling that she was aloof. Obviously he had a good thing going with green-eyed, blond-haired, flip and friendly Emily Summers. Why would he want to break that off?

But something didn't quite add up, and Beth, for the life of her, couldn't figure out what it was. . . .

Caprice Romances from Tempo

A CAPRICE ROMANCE

Two of a Kind
Susan Shaw

TEMPO BOOKS, NEW YORK

TWO OF A KIND

A Tempo Book/published by arrangement with
the author

PRINTING HISTORY
Tempo Original/February 1985

ISBN: 0-441-83432-9

Tempo Books are published by The Berkley Publishing Group,
200 Madison Avenue, New York, New York 10016.
Tempo Books are registered in the United States Patent Office.
PRINTED IN THE UNITED STATES OF AMERICA

Chapter One

Beth fumbled with her books. She transferred them to her left arm and slapped her right jean pocket, then transferred them to her right arm and slapped her left jean pocket. Where was her pencil?

With a sigh of resignation, she banged her books on the floor. The top one, Algebra, slid off. Beth bent over to straighten it back on the pile, and thought, What am I doing, signing up for this contest, anyway? Frank's crazy, making me promise to try out for everything so I can meet people and make friends. Signing up for a writing contest isn't going to help me get any closer to Ted Sealley.

Three months ago, during Christmas break, Beth and her parents moved to Cedar Island, Washington, a small island west of Seattle. Beth's brother Frank, a student at MIT, had said, "Join clubs and participate in things, Beth. That's the best way to meet people in a new school."

Easier said than done, Beth thought wryly. Little did Frank know how difficult it was to meet people, even though she had tried out for absolutely everything. First, she had auditioned for a part in the school play, *Peter Pan*. She hadn't even gotten the part of the dog! Then she'd painted a poster for the "Keep Washington Green" contest. Margot Sealley, Ted's sister, won.

Beth's heart pounded whenever she thought of Ted. But this time, she forced herself to continue down the list of her failures. She had auditioned for cheerleading, but fell over doing a cartwheel. The next week, she had tried out as scorekeeper for the swim team. But the first day at the pool, even though she smelled the caustic chlorine until her lungs ached, she had temporarily forgotten where she was and didn't remember to stop the watch in time. The swim coach fired her on the spot.

Last week, Rosie McNeil, her first and, so far, only friend at Cedar Island High, had persuaded Beth to try out for the track team. Beth went because she knew Ted Sealley would be there. She came in last place, which was bad enough, but she felt even worse when Ted smiled at her and said, "Better luck next time."

Next time, ha! thought Beth, wishing she could fall into a pit and come out in China. China would be better than Cedar Island. And with her black hair, dark eyes, olive complexion, and slight figure, she probably wouldn't look too much out of place.

"Howdy!"

Someone snapped their fingers. Beth blinked her eyes and saw red-haired Rosie. Miss Muscle herself.

"Howdy," Rosie said again. "Were you daydreaming?"

"Caught in the act," Beth said sheepishly.

"What's up?" Rosie asked in her quick, bright way. She was cute and compact. Her muscles seemed to ripple through her gray sweat pants and her gray-green sweatshirt.

"Nothing," said Beth, embarrassed. She didn't want to tell Rosie what she was doing, in case she failed again.

"In that case I gotta keep moving," Rosie said. "I didn't get any homework done last night."

"How come?"

"Same two reasons as always," Rosie said with a bright grin. "Track practice and Jens."

"In that order?" Beth smiled at her friend.

Rosie's hazel eyes twinkled. "Depends on the season," she said. "But since Coach has us working out every day, for once I'm thinking more of track than of Jens.'' She took two quick steps down the hall. "See you at lunch."

"See you," Beth said, watching Rosie's red ponytail with its bright yellow ribbon, until she disappeared down the crowded school hall.

A pencil, thought Beth as she stopped looking at Rosie, and dived into her purse. She curled her fingers around wadded balls of looseleaf paper, the beaded change purse Frank had sent from MIT for her seventeenth birthday in February, a crumbly package of corn nuts, a Wizard-of-Oz hanky, and the notebook where she recorded her dreams. No pencil.

"Are you signing up for this, too?" A cheery voice interrupted her thoughts.

Beth looked up and saw Emily Summers signing her name to the writing contest list. The top of Emily's E curled with a triple set of circles, as did the tail of the Y. Her name looked like it was surrounded by two spiral shells.

"Need a pen?" Emily handed her a mauve ballpoint.

When Beth tried to write her name on the paper pinned onto the wall, the ink gave out. Wouldn't you know it! "Just my luck," she said in a shaky voice and handed back the pen.

"No prob," Emily said, exchanging the pen for a pencil. The pencil was white with UNITED AIRLINES printed along the side in bold red letters.

"What are you going to write about?" Emily asked as Beth printed her name in small square letters.

"I don't know yet," Beth confessed, suddenly wondering what had possessed her to sign up.

"You and me both," Emily said. "I'm so busy I don't have time to think."

Emily suddenly bent forward as if to examine Beth closely. Beth looked up at her. Emily was at least five feet ten, about five inches taller than Beth. She had frizzy blond hair draped to her shoulders, and wore bright mauve lipstick and nailpolish. She was dressed in a mauve vest with its snaps undone down the front, a black blouse, and black-and-white-striped pants. Her eyes were emerald-green.

"I have just thought of something," Emily said in a dramatic voice.

Beth was left speechless and awed by Emily's presence.

"I didn't know you could write or I'd have asked you sooner. Can you come to Mrs. Atkinson's room after school and help us edit the school paper? There's some real airheads who submitted articles this month and you wouldn't believe the mess they made of their spelling and punctuation."

Before Beth had time to blurt, "But I can't spell," Ted Sealley appeared at Emily's elbow.

Beth was suddenly conscious that the snowflakes on the front of her wool sweater were covered with tiny fuzz balls. But when Ted grinned, she forgot the fuzz balls. She rested her feet against her books, trying to keep herself from floating away. Her brain went blank.

Ted was about two inches taller than Emily. He had blond straight hair, green eyes, a lean runner's face, and a single dimple that sunk so deep into his right cheek it looked as if it would appear as a bump on the other side of his face.

Beth looked at Ted's left cheek. It was smooth. Not a dimple. Not a blemish. But his right cheek . . . Beth squeezed her fingers over her thumbs, suppressing the urge to touch Ted's dimple with her finger.

Beth stared from Emily to Ted and felt hypnotized, as if a magician had escaped from a circus and come to Cedar Island High for the sole purpose of putting her under a spell.

"Good luck with the contest," Ted said.

I could use it, thought Beth. I haven't had any luck in anything since we moved to Cedar Island.

"I'm sure not programming myself to lose, Ted Sealley," Emily said, her green eyes flashing.

Beth looked down at the eraser on the end of Emily's United Airlines pencil and thought, I can erase my name, right now, before anyone else knows. Me compete with Emily Summers? How many times do I have to try something and lose before I give up?

"Don't tell anyone," Emily was saying in stage whisper, "but I'm such a poor sport, if I thought I was going to lose, I wouldn't bother trying."

"That's stupid," Ted said. "No one can win everything."

"What's the point of trying out for something if you think you're going to fail?" Emily retorted.

You said it, thought Beth, but she kept her mouth shut.

"Beth tried out for track team . . ." Ted said.

Oh, no, thought Beth, here it comes! Another one of my failures exposed to the world.

"I thought it was terrific of her. She wasn't afraid to try, even though she hadn't had any track training."

How do you know I hadn't had any training, thought Beth. Was it that obvious?

"That's okay for you," Emily said, gripping the lapels of her mauve vest as she shifted her glance from Ted to Beth.

"What's the big deal about winning?" Ted asked.

"I can't stand to lose." Emily pulled herself up until she looked as tall as Ted's six feet. She was obviously unhappy that he had called her stupid.

"I'll tell you something," Ted continued in a serious voice. "Once I stopped worrying about winning all my meets, I relaxed and enjoyed myself. The more I relaxed, the better my times were."

Beth looked at him. His words went round inside her head: ". . . big deal about winning . . . relaxed and enjoyed myself . . ."

"So why'd you say 'good luck'?" Emily retorted defensively.

Ted shrugged his shoulders. "Why not?"

"Oh, you!" Emily stamped her foot. She wore black clogs and the noise thudded above the rumble of students hurrying past to their classrooms. "Answer my question."

"I was just trying to make conversation." The muscles in Ted's lean face tightened. "So calm down, Emily!"

"I need all the luck I can get," Beth said, jumping in, hoping to smooth things over.

Ted's whole expression changed. He grinned at her, and his dimple deepened.

"You've got to stop talking in clichés, Ted Sealley," Emily interjected with a rapid fluttering of her eyelashes.

Unable to stand the way Emily was flirting with Ted, Beth

bent down and picked up her books from between her feet.

The warning bell rang for first period. Ted and Emily abruptly turned and hurried down the hall. Beth stared at their blond heads and wondered how two people forgetting to say good-bye could make her feel so low. She combed her bangs with her fingers, holding her head up high so nobody would be able to detect her hurt expression.

Suddenly both Ted and Emily turned around and walked back toward her. Beth noticed for the first time that Ted wore a green T-shirt with the word SUPERMAN printed across the front in white block letters.

"I can't go to the ASB meeting after school," Emily explained as soon as they were three feet from Beth. "I've *got* to go to Mrs. Atkinson's room to edit those articles for the paper."

"And Emily is ASB secretary," Ted said, "and . . ."

"And I was wondering," interrupted Emily . . .

"*We* were wondering," Ted said, grinning at Beth with that fantastic dimple and those incredible green eyes.

"If you could possibly fill in for me at the meeting," Emily said. "You know, read the minutes and take notes."

"Would you mind?" asked Ted.

"Please?" Emily asked. "I'll bring you last month's minutes at lunch and all you have to do is read them and then take notes on the new business. I don't mind writing them up. Unless you want to, that is."

As Emily and Ted stood waiting for her answer, Mr. George, the white-haired principal, came out of his office behind them and looked pointedly up at the clock above his door. A boy with horn-rimmed glasses and a briefcase darted past them. He was from Beth's first period Chemistry class and she knew she should be hurrying, too.

"Sure," Beth said quickly, her voice sounding high and strange. "Sure," she said again in her regular voice. "Glad to help."

"I knew you would," said Ted, grinning.

"I'll bring you the ASB book at lunch," said Emily.

"I'll meet you in Algebra," Ted said, "and we can walk down to the meeting together."

Algebra. Last period. How was she going to survive a whole day of classes until last period? Beth clutched her books to her chest and sped down the hall to the Chemistry lab. Maybe Cedar Island wasn't so bad after all!

Chapter Two

Lunch had been the loneliest time of the school day until two months ago when Beth had bumped into Rosie. Literally bumped into her, that is, as she walked into the library, planning to spend the lunch period hidden behind the bookshelves so that no one would see her eating alone.

"Howdy," Rosie had said after they had collided through the library door and straightened themselves. "You're new, aren't you?"

"Yes," Beth had said in a shaky voice.

"Come eat with me," Rosie had insisted in a friendly voice. "I want to hear all about the wide world that exists outside of Cedar Island."

Beth had eagerly accepted the cheerful invitation, and thus began their daily custom of eating lunch together.

Today Beth met Rosie at a small round table in the corner of the cafeteria.

"You look like you're walking on clouds. What's up?" Rosie said as Beth opened her paper sack and unwrapped her sandwich.

"Nothing," Beth said, concentrating on nibbling the lettuce that fringed her cheese sandwich. She was dying to tell Rosie about Ted but what if he was interested in Emily? She'd have to give up her feelings for him, and she didn't want to. It was too much fun to dream about him and wonder if she might have a chance.

"Didn't Mrs. Atkinson ask you to sign up for the writing contest?" persisted Rosie.

"Yes," Beth said.

"Well?" Rosie pressed, "did you?"

Beth nodded, imagining a picture of Garfield jumping out of her lunch sack. So the cat was out of the bag despite the fact that she definitely didn't want anyone to know.

"What're you going to write about?"

"I don't know."

"You've got lots of time to think about it," Rosie said cheerfully. "The deadline isn't until the end of April."

"How do you know?" Beth looked at Rosie in surprise.

"One thing you have to learn about Cedar Island High," Rosie said between mouthfuls of her Milky Way candy bar, "is that everyone knows everything about everyone and everything."

No way, thought Beth. No one's going to know how I feel about Ted.

"For example," Rosie continued, "I happen to know that half the high school girls cheer at the track meets, not because they particularly care that Cedar Island wins, but because they want to see Ted Sealley in shorts."

Beth tried to keep the startled look out of her eyes. Had Rosie been reading her mind? She wiped her mouth on her paper napkin and tried not to look too interested.

Then a thought occurred to her. Maybe Rosie was crazy about Ted, too. Beth cleared her throat and said, "What do you think of Ted?"

"I like him." Rosie crumpled up her candy wrapper. "Who doesn't?"

"Would you give up Jens if Ted asked you out?" Beth leaned across the table. Her forehead creased underneath her bangs.

"I doubt it," Rosie said. She flexed her fingers in and out, practicing, as she had once told Beth, for grabbing the relay baton. "But who knows? I've never had the opportunity to find out, and likely never will."

"What if you did have the opportunity to find out?" Beth struggled with the words, but she just had to know.

Rosie looked at her curiously. "Jens and I have been an item since the sixth grade," she said slowly. "I can't imagine dating anyone else, even someone as nice as Ted Sealley."

Beth sat back in her chair, her shoulders relaxing.

"Don't get me wrong," Rosie continued and Beth tightened up again. "I mean—" Rosie's face flushed the color of her hair "—Jens and I sort of plan to get married someday."

"That's great!" Beth cried with a grin.

Rosie, still with a red face, put a finger to her lips and said, "Don't tell a soul or I'll . . ." She made a chopping karate motion with the side of her right hand against the table.

"I promise," Beth said, "and if there's one thing I'm good at, it's keeping a promise."

"I knew I could trust you," Rosie said. "You just look like that type of person."

Beth smiled and, since she couldn't think of anything to say, said nothing.

Rosie's lunch always consisted of a Milky Way bar and a pint of milk. Nothing else. She had finished both so she chatted away about Jens and his uncle's fishing boat while Beth chewed her sandwich and drank her can of apple juice. Beth interrupted with, "Oh, how neat!" or "What fun!" every so often, to let Rosie know she was listening, but privately she was thinking about the afternoon and the upcoming chance to get to know Ted better. I can't goof up, she thought, and felt herself tighten with nervousness.

When Beth finished eating, they pushed back their chairs and, still chatting, Rosie led the way out of the lunchroom.

"Hey! Beth Hamilton!"

Beth swiveled her head toward the far side of the room. Emily Summers stood on a chair, waving her arm in a circle.

"What's that about?" Rosie asked, raising her eyebrows.

"I have to take Emily's place at the ASB meeting," Beth said, trying to make it sound as if it were an ordinary event. "I better go see what she wants."

"I'll talk to ya later, then," Rosie said. "Call me tonight and let me know how the meeting goes. You'll get to sit beside you know who."

What on earth could Rosie have meant by that remark, Beth thought all the way across the large room until she reached Emily's table. She recognized several kids, including the boy with thick horn-rimmed glasses who was the smartest student in her Chemistry class. Ted wasn't at the table. At least he doesn't eat lunch with Emily, thought Beth, and then corrected herself. At least not today.

"Here's the ASB notebook," Emily said, handing Beth a thick green binder with CEDAR ISLAND HIGH written in yellow script across the front.

"Thanks," Beth said, flipping through the pages to look for the minutes of the last meeting.

"Thank *you*," said Emily. "You've saved my life."

I doubt that, thought Beth, but out loud she said, "Anytime."

"You mean it?" Emily curled her finger through one of her tight blond curls.

"Sure." On the last page, Beth found the minutes, written in Emily's flowery style. "I never do anything after school."

"Gee," Emily said, "and all this time I thought you were practicing the violin or taking ballet lessons, or doing something exotic like that."

"Me?" Beth widened her eyes in surprise. "I don't do anything like that." In fact I do nothing, she thought, except study and wish I could make a few more friends and find an easy way to get involved in things at Cedar Island High.

"What'd'ya know," said Emily, in her theatrical voice. "Just you wait. We'll get you so busy you won't know what hit you. You'll wish you *were* practicing the violin every day for five hours."

"Or the drums." A Japanese boy poked his head between them. He tapped his fingers on both Emily's and Beth's shoulders, as if they were two sets of bongos.

"Knock it off, drummer boy," Emily said sharply, wriggling her shoulder.

Beth didn't mind the light tapping on her shoulder at all. It was sure better than being totally ignored! But he spun around on his heel and left after Emily's remark.

"Hey, Ray, come on back," Emily ordered.

Ray barged out of the lunchroom as if he didn't hear, but surely, thought Beth, everyone in the lunchroom could hear Emily's loud voice.

"All I was going to do was introduce you to him," Emily said in such a hurt tone that Beth felt sorry for her.

"That's okay," Beth said quickly. "You can do it next time."

"Humph," said Emily, majestically tossing her head. "If there is a next time!"

Beth felt embarrassed. Emily seemed to be putting on a show, and she didn't want to be in the audience. She closed the book and was trying to think of a way to get out of there when Emily said in a normal voice, "Do you think you'll be able to read my writing okay?"

"I'm sure I will," Beth said politely.

"Ted will help you if you have trouble," Emily said, quickly picking up her books from the table, and starting for the door.

Beth followed. Of course Ted will help me, she thought sarcastically. He's probably been reading Emily's writing since they were kids in grade school.

Oh rats, Beth cursed silently, as an awful sinking feeling fluttered in the pit of her stomach. Why did I say I'd go to the meeting? It's only going to make me feel worse.

Chapter Three

Is Ted going steady with Emily, or isn't he? Beth wondered as she was walking down the hall to Algebra. She thought, Even if he isn't going with Emily, why would he want to go with me? I'm nobody special.

She pulled open the door to the classroom in front of Phillip Predo who swooped off his black beret and bowed deeply to let her pass. Beth grinned at him, missing an opportunity to see if Ted was already in his customary seat in the back of the room.

By now Beth felt too embarrassed to obviously turn and search out Ted in the back row of the classroom, so she took her seat in the front row and watched Mr. Ives, the teacher, sitting like a statue behind his desk.

Mr. Ives had a crew cut and wore wool pleated pants that looked like they had been tailored in the fifties. He had also studied for his PhD in Physics, Rosie had told Beth, but gave it up to return to Cedar Island and teach high school. He was an excellent teacher so normally Beth had no trouble paying attention.

But today everything was different. Her mind drifted to the back of the room where Ted sat. As she looked slightly sideways, she could see his long legs spread alongside his small desk. His elbows were bent and his hands cupped, supporting his chin. His white-blond hair flopped around his face.

To put it bluntly, thought Beth, he's totally gorgeous.

"Beth Hamilton?"

Sharply, shattering the wisps of her dreams, Beth heard her name. Rats! Where were we?

"Do you have the answer for us?" Mr. Ives continued.

What answer? Beth tried to focus.

"See me after class," Mr. Ives boomed.

Trust me to screw up, Beth fumed while her face flushed. So much for taking notes at the ASB meeting. Fouled up my one chance to be with Ted Sealley. I knew it! I knew I'd goof up somehow.

Phillip Predo waved his beret in the air. When Mr. Ives didn't notice, he called out an answer.

Mr. Ives smashed his fist down on his desk. "No talking," he shouted. His dark eyes seemed to bore into each individual in the classroom. "If I want you to speak, Mr. Predo, I'll call on you," he shouted again.

Phillip pulled his beret down over his eyes.

Beth squirmed, and for the rest of the period, she forced herself to pay attention.

After the bell, Beth's hands started to sweat. She snapped her looseleaf papers back in her binder and tried to think of ways to stall for time. As people rushed out of the room, Beth slowly slid out of her seat, looking down at her books.

"I'll wait for you outside," Ted said, coming up behind her. "He won't keep you long."

"What if I have detention?" Beth asked, holding out the ASB notebook. "You better get someone else to read the minutes." Her lips trembled as she said the words, and she quickly bit her bottom lip.

Ted shook his head. "I'm sure you don't have detention," he said in a soothing voice. "Ives may be gruff but he doesn't give detentions just because someone was daydreaming."

Daydreaming! Oh, no! thought Beth. What if Ted realized I was daydreaming about him? She got so flustered she could hardly stand still, and found herself slipping her feet in and out of her loafers, one after the other.

Ted bent over and whispered, "If you do get detention, just tell the old bulldog that you've got to go to the ASB meeting and you'll have to take it another day. Tell him you're absolutely essential. We can't have the meeting without you.''

Beth giggled nervously. She couldn't help but laugh when Ted called Mr. Ives a bulldog. He did, in fact, look like a bulldog. Unfortunately, like a bulldog who just might bite.

"I'll wait outside for you," Ted said, and flicked his fingers in a quick salute.

Beth gripped her books and trembled a little as she walked to the front of the room.

Mr. Ives sat at his desk, his hands folded. "It occurred to me that you might not have heard of the Math Club," Mr. Ives said, talking in a calm, ordered voice. "We're grooming ourselves for a state tournament at the end of May. I hope you might consider entering."

Enterer, that's me, thought Beth. She opened her mouth and, stuttering, said, "Well, sir, I don't know, sir . . . I mean, sir, I space out sometimes, and I doubt if I'm good enough to enter a competition."

"I am quite aware that you don't always pay attention," Mr. Ives said with a dark look, "but that doesn't mean you're not good at mathematics. You are, in fact, getting the highest marks in this class."

Beth raised her eyebrows and permitted herself a small grin. So Mr. Ives wasn't going to chew her out after all!

"Tell me," Mr. Ives said kindly, "why would you get the idea that you weren't good enough at mathematics?"

Remembering that Ted was waiting outside the door, Beth said quickly, "I'm not really serious about math, I guess."

"Do you think," Mr. Ives said with infuriating slowness to his words, "that because you aren't serious about math, it means you aren't good at it? I don't understand."

"What I mean to say," Beth said, trying to control her nervousness, "is that I didn't think that something you didn't do seriously was something that you would want to compete with everyone in. It would spoil the fun of it." That's that, thought Beth, ready to race out the door toward Ted.

Mr. Ives said, "There's absolutely nothing wrong with having fun with math, and why not think of it as competing with yourself, rather than the rest of the world. Enter the competition for the very reasons that you stated, because you don't want to take math seriously.''

Beth felt very frustrated listening to all this. All she wanted to do was dash out the door.

''Math obviously isn't difficult for you,'' Mr. Ives droned on, ''but for some strange reason you think it will spoil the fun by having to compete. Why?''

Beth could not answer him.

Mr. Ives lowered his dark eyebrows and continued in a serious tone, ''As a matter of fact, the best kind of mathematician, in fact the best kind of competitor there is, is one who is confident of the material and isn't so uptight about winning that they freeze and can't think straight.''

Beth thought of what Ted had told Emily that morning. Mr. Ives seemed to be repeating the idea almost word for word.

''In the Math Club we're looking for people who aren't afraid to think creatively about mathematics,'' Mr. Ives said, although Beth was listening with half an ear, trying to figure out how to escape. '' . . . to play with numbers and ideas,'' finished Mr. Ives.

Despite her distraction, Mr. Ives's words finally sunk in and Beth blurted out, ''I know what you're saying, sir, because my brother Frank's like that. He loves figuring things out. He's really the reason I'm good in math.''

What am I doing? thought Beth. Bragging!

''I didn't mean to brag, sir,'' she added quickly. ''What I mean is . . .'' she paused and searched her mind, wanting to express the thought right. ''I mean, my brother always insisted on helping me with arithmetic when I started school and he just kept on. He said it would hurt the family honor to have me do poorly in mathematics.''

''Just because you accept your own abilities, doesn't mean you're bragging,'' Mr. Ives said, grinning so widely that his plump cheeks were creased by his thick lips.

Bzzzzz!

Beth jumped. She inched backward toward the door, dying

to get out of the room and be with Ted. The sharp whine came
from the region of Mr. Ives's wrist. He lifted his suit sleeve
and exposed a watch with a dial half the size of Beth's palm.

"Now what was that for?" he said absentmindedly, pushing in a pin-sized button, stopping the noise. "Oh, yes. Good
thing I set my alarm. I might have forgotten."

He pushed back his chair and looked at Beth through his
dark, penetrating eyes. "It's been a pleasure talking to you,
Miss Hamilton. I hope you will give the Math Club your
utmost consideration. You have an excellent mathematical
mind and I would enjoy working with you on a more ad-
vanced level than what we are obliged to cover in class."

He pushed back his chair and led the way to the door. "It is
Tuesday, isn't it?" he asked, turning to Beth, his hand on the
doorknob.

She nodded her head, bewildered. "Tuesday, the twen-
tieth of March," she said.

"Math Club meets every Tuesday in the Commons," Mr.
Ives said. "Are you able to come today?" He held the door
open for Beth.

"I'm sorry I can't," Beth said, glancing over to Ted who
sat propped against the wall with his math book on his knees.
"I have a previous commitment."

Ted shut his book and straightened his long legs.

"In that case I hope you'll come next week," Mr. Ives
said. "I'm sure you'll enjoy the club and you don't *have* to
compete if you don't want to."

He left Beth and padded down the hall.

"Everything okay?" Ted asked when he joined Beth.

"You were right!" Beth grinned with relief and with the
excitement of being alone with Ted. "No detention, but I'm
sorry he talked so long. I couldn't get away."

"What did he want?" Ted asked.

"He asked me to join the Math Club."

"That's a big deal," Ted said. "You're lucky, you know.
He's never asked me."

"Really?" Beth raised her eyebrows.

"Mr. Ives thinks one bad apple can spoil the bunch so he

only asks the best students to join the Math Club.''

Beth grinned to herself at Ted's cliché, and stared down the hall to avoid looking at him. She was afraid that if she didn't avert her eyes from his, she'd be hopelessly riveted to them forever.

Ted walked beside her. Several times Beth moved closer to him in an effort to avoid being bumped by kids hurrying to catch the school buses. She loved the feeling of being next to him, but hoped he didn't think she was flirting with him. Searching her mind for something to say, she blurted out, "I'm a dunce in math compared to my brother Frank."

Ted stopped and looked at her curiously. "Do you always compare yourself to your brother?"

Beth nodded.

"My sister Margot and you ought to get together," he said. "She's always comparing herself to me though I keep telling her not to."

Beth laughed. "You're talking just like *my* brother," she said.

"Does your brother also tell you to be yourself and not to worry about anybody else?"

Beth nodded her head up and down in an exaggerated motion. She felt her short black hair tickle the sides of her cheek.

"Does he tell you to be the best *you* can be?" continued Ted.

Beth nodded and grinned up at him. Ted grinned back. His dimple deepened and Beth was glad, totally glad, that he was Margot's brother and not her own.

"I'd like to meet your brother sometime," Ted said. "He must be pretty neat to have a sister like you."

Beth looked up at him, startled. Then she smiled. Yes, Frank was pretty neat. She still missed him, though he hadn't lived at home on a regular basis since he had enrolled in MIT five years ago.

"Here we are," Ted said, taking her arm and guiding her through a maze of rooms to the right of the principal's office.

At his touch, Beth's knees shook. All her thoughts, all the worries that she would goof, say something wrong, or appear stupid, dropped behind her like a load of tin cans. As she floated on air, all she could think of was Ted, and how absolutely, totally, miraculously wonderful it was to have his hand on her arm.

Chapter Four

"The meeting will now come to order." Ted clapped his hands twice.

Ray, the same Japanese student whom Emily wanted to introduce to Beth at lunch, was drumming his fists on the Formica table. The girl next to him nudged his elbow, signaling him to stop. The large group hushed.

"This is Beth Hamilton," Ted said, indicating Beth who sat beside him. "She's taking over for Emily today. Will you read the minutes, Beth?"

Beth read the minutes from the last meeting, pausing only twice to get Ted's help in deciphering Emily's curly letters. Then the major business meeting began.

Beth quickly scribbled notes on a clean looseleaf paper she took from her own folder, getting down the jist of what people said. Finally Ted, in his presidential voice, asked, "Does anyone want to move that we sponsor a May Day Dance?"

"I so move," Ray said.

"I second," said a girl who wore heavy red lipstick and looked about twenty-five years old.

"Moved by Ray Nishimoto and seconded by Gloria Davis that we sponsor a May Day Dance," Ted said.

Beth wrote furiously while she tried to push the resounding question—Will Ted ask me?—out of her head.

"How much do we have in the treasury?" Ted asked.

The boy from Beth's Chemistry lab opened his briefcase and took out a yellow-lined sheet of paper. He adjusted his glasses and, after studying the paper for a few seconds, said, "We've got zilch in the treasury. We went broke after the Christmas Party because we had to pay so much for the Tracers to come over from Seattle."

"And they weren't even that great a band," Ray Nishimoto said, drumming his fingers on the table as if to emphasize his point.

"They stank," someone else said bluntly.

"I have an idea," the boy with the horn-rimmed glasses said.

"Eggie has the floor," said Ted. After everyone stopped talking, Ted leaned over Beth's shoulder and whispered into her ear, "That's Tom Bellga, but we've called him Eggie since the sixth grade when he wrote the best paper in class. He's an egghead."

Don't I know it! thought Beth, remembering his brilliant experiments in Chemistry lab.

Tom Bellga announced, "My dad's fifties dance band might play for nothing. We'll solve the theme problem and the money problem at the same time. In fact, we might make money for a change."

Beth watched Ted look around the tightly packed room. There were twenty people in a space meant for ten. "Any discussion?" Ted asked after a moment of silence.

The walls bounced with noise.

"Hold it down," said Ted quietly. Miraculously, the room hushed.

He's a natural leader, thought Beth. He deserves to wear that SUPERMAN shirt. But just thinking those words to herself caused her to swallow a lump in her throat. What would he want with me? she thought. What would someone special like Ted Sealley want with a first-class failure like me?

People were talking from all directions. Beth swiveled her head, trying to get all the ideas listed. Then Ted called to the girl who had seconded the motion for the dance, and was now talking the loudest.

"What do you think, Gloria?" he asked.

"I think if it's a fifties theme I won't get to wear my new dress."

"You can wear whatever you want to the dance," Eggie said. "You don't *have* to come fifties."

"Then I'll feel out of place," Gloria whined.

I don't believe I'm hearing her talk like this, thought Beth. Gloria looks so grown-up yet she sounds like a six year old.

Ted pressed both hands on the table and leaned forward. "Are we ready for the motion?"

"Motion," several people concurred.

Ted nodded at Eggie who said, "I move that we ask Mr. Bellga and his fifties dance band to play for the May Day Dance at Cedar Island High, with the theme as the fifties."

"Second," Ray Nishimoto said.

"All in favor?" asked Ted.

Even Gloria Davis raised her hand.

I probably won't get to go, Beth thought dejectedly as she printed "Motion Passed," on the looseleaf sheet. No one will ask me, least of all Ted. He's probably already invited Emily! I'm sure they discussed the idea of the dance together.

"Will you talk to your dad?" Ted asked Eggie. "Let me know the answer tomorrow."

Tom nodded. His horn-rimmed glasses bobbed up and down his nose.

Ted spoke to a girl with long blond hair that almost reached her waist. "Will you be in charge of posters, Kit? I'm sure Margot will be glad to help."

"Sure," said Kit.

"Ray, can you get the food and punch arranged?"

Ray Nishimoto nodded his head and drummed the table with his pencil.

Oh, dear, thought Beth, watching him. That reminds me. I forgot to give Emily back her pencil. She probably thinks I'm never going to return it.

"I'll talk to the principal as soon as I hear if Mr. Bellga and his band can come," said Ted. "So hold off on the other arrangements until you hear from me."

"I move meeting dismissed," Ray Nishimoto said.

"Second," said Kit, the girl with the waist-length hair.

People started moving chairs and gathering their books. Beth's head buzzed as much with the new names and faces as it did with the presence of Ted. Every nerve in her body seemed aware of the fact that Ted's hands were pressed on the table, almost beside hers. If I inch my fingers over, I can touch his, she thought, wondering if she could pretend it was an accident.

"You did a good job," Ted said, reading her notes over her arm. "And your printing is so neat. Would you come again if Emily's busy?"

Would she come again? Beth looked up at Ted and smiled. For a moment their eyes met, but suddenly there was Tom "Eggie" Bellga, breaking the spell.

"Are you planning on joining the Math Club?" he said to Beth.

Beth almost jumped in her seat in surprise. How did he know? Maybe what Rosie said was true, that everyone knew everything about everybody on Cedar Island. "I don't know," she said. "I just heard about it from Mr. Ives."

"I'm going down to the Commons now," Eggie said. "Do you want to come?"

"I was going to offer you a ride home," Ted said, studying her closely. "But if you want to go to with Eggie, well . . ." his voice trailed off.

Beth thought quickly and then said to Ted, "Oh, I'd love a ride home." She turned to Eggie, "Sorry," she said, hoping she looked sorry although she felt joyful to be going home with Ted, "but I'd better get home. My mom usually expects me right after school." Since I never go anywhere or do anything, she added under her breath.

She pushed back her chair and walked out of the room with Ted and Eggie, carrying the green ASB notebook on top of her own pile of books.

Outside the door, Ted said, "How's it going for the State Math Competition this spring?"

"So-so," Eggie said. "Brandon's president and he's pretty formidable. Then there's me, who never does the equations the way they set them out, but usually gets the right answers."

Beth looked at Eggie with renewed interest. "I bet you'd like my brother," she blurted out.

"Oh, yeah?" Eggie said in a friendly voice. "Why do you say that?"

"He's at MIT in Pure Mathematics and he always used to figure out his own way to do the equations, too."

"I want to go to MIT," Eggie said, "but I'm thinking of studying something practical like Computer Science."

"I know what you mean," Beth said. "Frank's not even sure he'll be able to find a job when he gets his PhD in Pure Maths. But it doesn't seem to bother him. He's having so much fun with what he's studying now, that he doesn't even think about working."

"I'd sure like to talk with him," Eggie said. "Let me know if he ever comes to Cedar Island."

"Be glad to," Beth said, and for a few moments she wished Frank would come home, and be close enough to boost her confidence, as he always did.

Beth headed down the hall between Ted and Eggie and was just about to turn to Ted and say something, when Eggie said, "What do you think of our dance plans?"

"They sound great! My mom has a pink felt poodle skirt that she's saved since she was in high school, and I've been dying for a chance to wear it."

Rats! she thought, wishing she could swallow the words. I sound like I'm trying to weasel an invitation, and it's not Eggie I want to ask me out, it's Ted.

"Gee," Eggie said in a pleased voice. "I'm glad you like the idea. I thought someone like you would want a professional type band."

"Didn't your dad used to play professionally?" Ted asked.

And at the same time Beth thought, What does he mean, someone like me? He doesn't even know who I am, or what I'm like!

Eggie was saying, "My dad used to earn his living playing in a band, but when he got burned out by all the late nights and the traveling to gigs, he gave it up and went to work for the telephone company. Now he only plays in the band in his spare time.''

"His dad's band is terrific," said Ted to Beth. "They always play in the Fourth of July parade and gather up all the Sunday musicians on the Island to join them."

"Including you know who," Eggie said, pointing a finger at Ted.

Beth stopped at her locker. With her hand on her lock, she turned her head around to look at Ted, glad to finally have a chance to talk directly to him. "What do you play?"

"I plunk around on a ukulele sometimes," Ted said. "Nothing exciting."

"He won the Fifth Grade Talent Show playing the ukulele," Tom said. "Don't let him put you on."

"I only won because I wore overalls and a Huck Finn straw hat," Ted said, laughing a deep, contagious laugh.

Beth avoided looking at his dimple, and thought, Why do they always talk about winning something? I'm sick of never winning anything. She spun her combination lock and flung open her locker. She slipped on her navy blue down jacket and turned around to see Eggie breakdancing down the hall. When he reached the end of the hall, he called, "Hope to see you next Tuesday in Math Club, Beth."

"Don't forget to ask your dad about playing for the dance," Ted called back.

Eggie swung his briefcase up and down, waving good-bye.

Funny, thought Beth as she and Ted walked out the front door of the school. In my other school, kids might cut Eggie out or call him weird. Here they seem to value him. Nobody looks down on him because he's different. In my other school, they'd reject him simply because he carries a briefcase!

"Do you play an instrument?" Ted said, interrupting Beth's thoughts.

"My mother sings in the church choir," said Beth, "but that's all the musical talent anyone in my family has."

Ted touched her elbow. "I'm glad you didn't go to Math

Club today. I've been looking forward to driving you home.''

Beth blinked her eyes. Am I hearing correctly? she wondered. Is this Superman really talking to me?

Beth walked beside Ted across the school grounds, feeling as if she were walking in a dream. It simply couldn't be true. But when she took a deep breath, and smelled the damp wind and soggy ground, she could see clearly that there she was on the asphalt parking lot, and that was, indeed, Ted Sealley opening the door of a 1949 Plymouth for her to climb in.

Chapter Five

Beth climbed into the Plymouth and immediately wondered, How close do I dare sit to Ted without his thinking I'm being pushy or forward? She solved the problem by dumping her books between her and the driver's seat.

Ted got into his side and started the engine, which sounded like a clap of thunder.

"I need a new muffler," he said, grinning at her.

"You're lucky you have a car," Beth said.

"Don't I know it," Ted said. "Especially on this small rock. I can't stand riding the school bus."

"What do you mean by 'rock'?" Beth asked.

"That's what a lot of us kids call Cedar Island," Ted explained with a twinkle in his green eyes. "Sometimes it seems like a rock out in the middle of nowhere. Same old faces, same old things to do. One small movie theater, two dinky restaurants. Let me tell you, it can get pretty boring."

"At least you know people," Beth blurted out before she realized what she was saying. "It's sort of awful . . ."

"If you don't know anybody?" Ted finished her sentence.

Beth nodded. She bit her bottom lip and wished she'd never opened her mouth.

"Coming to Cedar Island High must be a little like trying to punch your way into a sealed box," Ted said thoughtfully. "I never thought about it, but I bet it is. Especially since most of us have lived here all our lives, and our parents, in many cases, grew up here, too.''

Beth remained quiet, too angry with herself for revealing her feelings to say anything else.

"Well," Ted continued, driving the Plymouth out of the parking lot, "we're just going to have to do something about you."

"I guess we will!" Beth responded in a mock-cheerful voice, not knowing whether to laugh or cry. For a split second, she wished she could throw her books to the floor and sit right next to Ted. It felt so good to be able to tell her troubles to someone her own age and feel as if she were really being understood.

"There's someone I want you to meet," Ted said softly. "She's one of my favorite people."

She? Beth thought, squeezing her knuckles. Probably Ted's girl friend. I'm a fool to think he'd be interested in me. I might as well give up on him right now. In another split second, Beth wished she could jump out of the car and walk the four miles home.

She repressed the urge by studying the heavy overcast sky. Dark clouds seemed to be dropping lower and lower, covering the treetops like a thick, gray blanket.

"Penny for your thoughts," Ted said, turning left off High School Road to drive south on Cross Island Road.

There was no way Beth was going to tell him the truth. Thinking quickly, she said, "I was thinking about how everyone I meet at Cedar Island High seems to be a success in something or other, but I keep trying out for things and never seem to get anywhere."

"It's only because you haven't found the thing that's right for you," Ted said encouragingly. "Everyone's good at something."

"I'm not so sure about that," Beth said quietly, studying her short-clipped fingernails.

"What about math?"

"What about it?"

"You're good at that."

"That doesn't count."

"Why not?"

"It's not really what I'm talking about," Beth said.

"Explain."

When they reached the long arm of the bay that dipped into the center of Cedar Island, Ted turned right, and drove down to the head of the bay. The water was dark and turbulent. White-capped waves, like large rooster tails, crested from one point of land to the other.

"Everyone here seems to have an abundance of self-confidence," explained Beth, after a long pause. "They're not afraid of trying anything. And besides that, they always seemed to succeed at whatever they try."

"If I had to leave Cedar Island High right now and go to another school somewhere else," Ted said, "I'd be scared out of my mind. I'd probably lose whatever self-confidence I have, and end up a dough-head."

"I was scared stiff to move here," Beth admitted.

"Really?" Ted looked at her in surprise. "I'd have never guessed. It looked like it didn't bother you a bit."

Beth shook her head. I don't believe it, she thought. How could anyone say that when I've totally fallen apart, really ready to dig myself into a huge hole and hide.

"I'll tell you a secret," Ted said, "if you promise not to tell anyone I told you."

"Promise," Beth said automatically.

"Everyone at school was kind of afraid of you, because you seemed so, well, aloof, and well . . ." he paused.

"Go on," Beth urged, her voice shaking. Aloof? she thought. Is he talking about me? All I've been trying to do is keep my head up so I don't break down and sob in the middle of the hall.

"You won't hate me for saying this?" Ted said, moving his right hand off the steering wheel and onto Beth's school books.

Beth shook her head.

"It seemed as if you felt you were better than the rest of us."

Beth's face flushed as she swallowed a lump in her throat. In a way it was ironic, Beth thought. How could anyone think

that she was better than everyone else when 999 percent of
the time she felt like a total failure.

"You aren't mad, are you?" Ted asked anxiously.

The tone of his voice caught her attention. Before Beth
knew what she was doing she had her hand on Ted's shoulder
and was patting it. "Of course I'm not mad," she said,
reassuring him as well as herself. "If you only knew . . ."

"Knew what?" Ted asked. The car seemed to splutter and
then Ted gunned the engine. Beth wished she could roll back
her words and start again. She pulled her hand away abruptly,
upset that she had revealed her feelings again.

"Knew how I really felt the past three months at school,"
Beth went on slowly, choosing the words carefully. "It just
shows how different the face one puts on to the world is, than
what is really happening inside."

"I hope," Ted declared as he started to drive slowly down
a side road, "that you feel that you don't have to put on a
mask at school and can just be yourself. I think that your real
self is a very fine person."

Beth felt like a million dollars.

"And now," Ted continued, "you are about to meet my
favorite woman. And I have the feeling that she's going to
like you one heck of a lot."

Just great, thought Beth. I suppose I should feel pleased
that Ted wants to introduce me to his favorite woman! Beth
blinked hard and forced herself to keep smiling. But somehow she could not bring herself to feel glad that Ted liked her
enough to introduce her to his girl friend.

Chapter Six

The car swerved back and forth as Ted drove around potholes in a long, rutted dirt road. Sheep grazed in a fenced pasture on one side of the road, and a creek rustled on the other side. Ted rounded a sharp corner and on a small knoll ahead of them, stood a two-story white Victorian house. A huge verandah circled the house, and by the wide front steps, a stooped woman with gray hair waved.

"I heard you coming," she called when Ted parked beside a small shed on the opposite side of the road from the house.

Ted jumped out, but Beth hesitated.

"Come and meet Alice," Ted called as he hugged the old woman.

Where's his favorite girl friend, thought Beth, trying her best not to appear curious, but feeling very awkward and uncertain.

"Alice Goddard, Beth Hamilton," introduced Ted, grinning from one to the other.

"Hello," Beth greeted, holding out her hand.

Alice's hand was gnarled but firm.

"Pleased to meet you," Alice said as she moved toward the shed. "Are you the folks living in the Kawaguchis' old place?"

"Yes," Beth said, feeling very uncomfortable with the thought that total strangers knew where she lived.

"Welcome, welcome," said Alice, "and give my welcome to your mother and dad. Old Mr. Kawaguchi was a good friend of mine, and I hope you folks will be, too.''

"Thank you,'' Beth said, feeling immediately at ease with Alice's friendly enthusiasm.

"Let me show you something,'' Alice said, climbing onto a bale of hay, then indicating for Beth to do the same. Ted was tall enough to peer over the narrow opening between the slanted roof and the sides of the shed.

Lying in a bundle of hay was a large white ewe. Her huge belly jiggled with motion as if several baby lambs were inside, trying to kick their way out. The ewe snorted, stretching out her long, pointed black nose at them.

"She's fussy today,'' Alice said, motioning them away from the pen. "Feels something in the air.''

"Is she having babies?'' Beth asked.

"Next weekend, I think,'' Alice said. "Come on down and see them.''

"Oh!'' Beth said, clapping her hands like a little kid. "I'd love to.''

Alice smiled up at her and Beth noticed how bright and clear her old eyes looked.

"Have you got time for a quick pot of tea?'' Alice asked, putting a gnarled hand on Ted's arm. "You've got a few minutes before the storm builds up.''

Ted raised his eyebrows at Beth. She nodded, but thought, Great, now I get to go inside and see his girl friend.

"Race you to the porch,'' Ted said. Beth charged ahead, her loafers flapping loosely. After twisting her foot on a large stone she stepped out of her left shoe and hopped forward on her uninjured foot. As Ted caught her arm, she felt tingles spark through her. I wouldn't mind stumbling all over the place, she thought, to fall into Ted's arms!

"Don't let that boy egg you on,'' Alice said when she caught up to them. "He's never missed a chance to race since he was knee-high to a tad chuck.''

"He can beat me anytime,'' Beth blurted out. "I'm such a klutz.''

"Don't put yourself down,'' Ted scolded, wagging a long

finger in her face. "I don't like people who put themselves down."

Tough, thought Beth, talking to Ted under her breath. Why would you like me anyway? Replacing her loafer and hunching her shoulders, she limped behind Alice into a warm farm kitchen, expecting at any moment to see someone as gorgeous as Emily, sitting at the kitchen table.

Beth stopped short and looked around the kitchen with her mouth agape. It looked like a picture of a kitchen in a book on pioneers. Bunches of herbs hung from the high ceiling; jars of dried apples and plums stood in a row on an oak counter; a copper kettle steamed from a wood stove that had MONARCH written in chrome across the front.

Ted held out a high-backed chair and Beth sat down, feeling as if she had been transported in time to an earlier and simpler age. Alice cut thick slices of rich, dark fruitcake, setting them on a pink china plate on the table. She pulled several dried leaves from one of the bunches hanging from the ceiling, and dropped them into a brown teapot which she filled with boiling water from the copper kettle. Then she covered the teapot with a knitted blue tea cozy.

"I haven't seen you since your mother . . ." Alice said, her words trailing off as she poured the pale green tea into three pink cups with matching saucers.

Beth looked quickly from Alice to Ted. His jaw tightened.

"Didn't mean to bring it up," Alice apologized as she handed him and Beth their cups of tea.

"That's okay," said Ted. "I should be able to talk about it by now."

"Takes time," Alice said. "Be nice to yourself and don't feel like you have to rush anything. Grief takes a long time." Alice turned to Beth and asked, "Would you like some honey in your mint tea?"

"No thanks," said Beth, sipping the steaming hot brew. "It's delicious just as is."

"I agree," Alice said. "But that honey we got last fall was mighty special. I think our bees worked overtime."

"Do you raise bees?" asked Beth, although in the back of

her mind she was wondering what had happened to Ted's mother and why Alice had mentioned grief.

"The bees raise themselves," said Alice with a chuckle. "But I do get in there and take something else that they raise. Honey, that is!"

"I'd love to try a spoonful," Beth said shyly.

"Just the kind of person I like," Alice said, dipping a silver spoon into a ceramic pot, which was shaped like a round bee hive.

Alice twisted the spoon and held it to Beth's mouth.

"Delicious," Beth said, licking the spoon clean. "What kind is it?"

"Mixed flower," Alice said proudly.

"Alice has the best honey on the island," informed Ted.

"Old Mr. Evans has the best fireweed honey," Alice conceded. "Of course he's got that burned field next to him with all the fireweed on it. But if I do say so myself, mine is the best mixed-flower honey on Cedar Island."

Beth, at that moment, felt light-years away from Bethesda, Maryland, and her old school. She felt warm and completely at home in Alice's old-fashioned kitchen. Nothing seemed to matter anymore except the taste of honey. In these friendly surroundings, it seemed easy to forget her worries about making friends and fitting in at Cedar Island High. But suddenly remembering what Ted had said, she peered into the adjoining living room, expecting to see a gorgeous woman getting ready to make an entrance. There was no one there.

"How's Dad's business?" Alice was saying.

"Busy," said Ted. "And that reminds me, he's got a School Board meeting tonight, and I was supposed to get home and fix dinner early."

While Alice and Ted were talking, Beth relaxed and stared out the window at a broad vegetable garden partially covered with dead brown corn stalks. Suddenly, cutting through her daydreams, a brilliant white light flashed across the sky.

"One. Two. Three," Alice counted slowly, and then came the thunderous, deafening roar as if a bomb had exploded.

"Three miles away," Ted said, quickly finishing his tea. "We'd better go."

"The March lion has finally roared," Alice said, grinning. "Come back next week and we'll have March lambs—literally."

Beth grinned despite her uneasy feelings about the weather. The air had an ominous stillness and felt weighted, motionless as they went out onto the verandah.

"My, oh, my," Alice said, shaking her gray head. "We're in a real low pressure area, so we're going to get the brunt of the storm. Don't forget to bring up some water from the well before the pump goes off."

Beth thought of the electric pump in the small pumphouse adjacent to her house, and wondered what Alice was talking about. The electric pump worked fine, so there was never any problem with water.

Ted bent down and hugged Alice. "Thanks," he said.

"Hurry along," said Alice. "Don't dawdle." She winked at Beth, who immediately wondered, What did she mean by that?

"Thanks for the tea," Ted called out the car window.

"Come again, Beth," Alice called. "And you, too, Ted. Love to Dad and Margot."

Beth smiled to herself and thought what fun it would be to talk to Alice about the old days. Maybe write a story about her for the writing contest? Suddenly she remembered that she hadn't met Ted's favorite woman. Unless . . . unless Ted meant gray-haired Alice with the stooped shoulders. If Alice is his favorite woman, thought Beth, with mounting excitement, maybe I've got a chance with him. Maybe I do!

Chapter Seven

"Do you know where I live?" Beth asked as Ted reached the end of Alice's long rutted driveway.

"Kawaguchi's?"

"Yes." Beth had become tense since the weather had changed abruptly. "Does it get like this very often?" she asked.

"Every spring," Ted said, "and everything usually breaks down. It gives you the feeling of what the island used to be like before Thomas Edison."

"It feels really weird," Beth said, gripping her hands together.

"No big deal," Ted said, looking at her carefully. "Not to worry." He turned right and headed to the south end of the island.

"I bet you know where everyone on this island lives," Beth commented.

"Used to," Ted agreed, "before the Trident submarine base went in over on Hood Canal and a bunch of new families moved up from California."

"And all this time I thought I was the only new person at Cedar Island High," Beth said warmly, feeling more secure.

"You're the only one who's come since Christmas," said Ted. "But there's a couple of new guys in our senior class who moved to the island in September, and one in your year who moved in November.''

I bet they fit in better than I do, Beth mused, squeezing her hands in her lap, trying to keep the sides of her mouth from turning down.

Dust from the edges of the black-topped road curled across the two lanes like a jump rope. Dried brown leaves bounced over the dust coils like gnomes playing the old skipping song, ''Bluebells, Cockleshells, Eevy Ivy Over.''

Ted turned his car into Beth's driveway, otherwise known as the Kawaguchi driveway. Mr. Kawaguchi was an artist who did a lot of sculpture. When he sold the house to the Hamiltons, he had said, ''I couldn't stand to live in a box. That's why the house is such an odd shape.''

Windows jutted out here and there, some were triangles, some were bay windows with seats, and one was a very unusual octagon-shape near the dining–kitchen table. Having the windows extend past the shaked sides of the house meant the house received lots of sunshine. But it seemed to Beth that the sun seldom shone, and if there wasn't rain, there was always the prospect of rain. Often the clouds lay so low to the ground that she felt that if she were only six inches taller, she could punch them and they would burst.

Ted circled the driveway turnaround, and pulled up in front of the pyramid-shaped porch. As they passed the old arbutus tree, it creaked and groaned in the strong wind.

''Thanks for the ride, and everything,'' Beth said, not wanting to open the door. ''I . . .'' she paused and then plunged ahead. ''Thanks for suggesting I go to the ASB meeting, and for taking me to meet Alice. I really like her.'' Beth wanted to add, And I'm really glad to have had a chance to talk to you. But she didn't dare.

''I knew you'd like Alice,'' Ted said. Yet his hands tightly clutched the wheel of his Plymouth, and it seemed to Beth that he was either angry or sad. Was it something she had done or said? How did he *know* she'd like Alice? What kind of messages was she giving out, anyway?

''Is everything all right?'' Beth asked, wanting and needing to know if she had said anything to upset him.

"Sometimes I hate to go home!" The words burst out of Ted so suddenly that they crackled against Beth's ears.

"Why?" Beth took her hand off the door and turned sideways in the seat, pulling her knees up and tucking her right foot underneath her.

"Didn't anyone tell you?" Ted's hands gripped the steering wheel so hard his knuckles turned white.

Beth shook her head. Who was there to tell her, except Rosie. Rosie wasn't one to gossip, and wouldn't have told Beth anything about Ted unless she had asked.

Ted moved his right hand onto the gray plush of the front seat. Without really thinking about it, or knowing why she did it, Beth put her hand over the top of his and stroked his hand as if they had been friends for years.

"My mom passed away," Ted said hoarsely. "In November."

Beth curled her fingers through his and remained still, waiting for him to speak.

"Mom had cancer for a long time," Ted continued, "so it wasn't as if we didn't expect it, but still . . ."

"That doesn't make it any easier," Beth finished quietly.

"You bet." Ted clutched her hand as if he were clutching a life preserver. Beth wanted to move closer and put her arms around him, but suddenly she felt overwhelmingly shy.

"Sometimes I just hate going home, knowing that she's not going to be there," Ted said. He pulled his hand away from Beth's and pounded the steering wheel.

"I wish I could help," Beth said softly, wanting with all her heart to make things easier for him.

The car engine sputtered as Ted gunned the gas pedal. "I've gotta leave," he said with a deep sigh. "This weather's the pits."

Beth opened the door and slid out.

"Thanks!" Ted flicked his fingers in a quick salute.

For what? thought Beth, feeling totally inadequate for not comforting him. I didn't do anything.

But as she stood on the steps watching him drive away, Ted smiled sadly at her and his dimple deepened. And Beth suddenly didn't care whether Emily or any other woman had first dibs on him or not. She knew, without a question of doubt, that she was in love with Ted Sealley.

She watched the wind wrestle with the trees, and smash down on the ramshackle shed at the end of the yard, knowing that she should go inside, and that Mom would be wondering where she was. But she wanted these few minutes alone to think about what Ted had said about his mother. That's what he and Alice had been referring to, she realized. Alice must not have seen Ted since his mom died. Beth shook her head and felt achingly sad, although she also felt comforted by the fact that Ted had confided in her.

A gust of wind slammed against her face, bringing her back to the present. Beth darted through the inside porch, and, opening the main door, called, "Hi, Mom."

"Hi, honey." Mom stood at the sink grating carrots. "Next time you're going to be late, call me, okay?"

Beth nodded and leaned against Mom's broad back, putting her arms around Mom's waist.

Mom had short brown curls, a string of worry lines across her forehead, and a comfortable roll around her middle, which she covered with big floppy sweaters. No one in their right mind would call Mom fat, but every so often she went on a diet and got grouchy, and lost a few pounds, only to gain it back in her enthusiasm to cook again for her family.

Mom turned around and hugged Beth tightly. "I guess I've lived in the city too long. I couldn't help but worry about you, especially with this wind coming up all of a sudden."

As if in response, the world rumbled and cracked, and Beth trembled, thinking of Ted driving through the lightning storm. Mom bent over and took a package of raisins from the bottom cupboard.

"So how did you get home, sweetheart?" Mom stirred the raisins into the grated carrots for Beth's favorite salad.

"A kid from school." Beth opened the fridge door to get the mayonnaise for the salad, but also to hide her flushed expression from Mom.

"Would you like to elaborate, dear?"

"His name is Ted Sealley and he's president of the Associated Student Body." Beth hoped she said it in a normal, matter-of-fact voice.

"Does that mean he's a senior?" Mom ladled the mayonnaise into the salad.

"Yes." Feeling more composed, Beth related the events of the day.

"I'm really pleased," Mom said. "It's the first time anyone other than Rosie has asked you to do anything."

"Unless you count Mrs. Atkinson, the English teacher," Beth said. "She asked me to sign up for the writing contest."

"Did you?"

"If I hadn't," Beth said, wrinkling her nose and thinking of how odd it was that both Emily and Ted had stopped to talk to her, "I'd probably never have gone to the ASB meeting."

"It's funny how things happen, isn't it?" Mom said. "How things sometimes come together. I think you just have to keep trying, Beth Ann, and you'll soon have a nice group of friends like the ones you had to leave in Bethesda." She handed Beth the salad, and added, "My mother always used to say, 'You take your friends with you,' and by that she meant that if you have friends where you are, you'll have friends where you're going."

Beth set the big pottery bowl of salad on the table. As the wind howled, thick hail crashed through the trees and covered the ground. Beth crossed her arms and hugged herself, grateful that she was safe at home, but still concerned about whether Ted had arrived at his house.

"I wish I didn't have to go out tonight," Mom said. "This weather's frightening."

"Where are you going?" Beth took three blue placemats and set them on the teak table.

"There's a choir meeting at the church," Mom said.

Beth pushed her bangs away from her eyes, and said, "I thought your choir practice was on Thursdays."

"This is a special meeting to choose songs for the Easter service." Mom opened the oven door and sprinkled the top of the macaroni-and-cheese casserole with buttered bread crumbs.

Beth took out the cutlery, but before she finished setting the table, the sky split open. All the nooks and crannies of the house seemed to wobble separately before connecting together again.

"My word!" Mom stiffened. "I wish David were home. I don't like the thought of his riding the ferry in this weather."

Beth continued to stare out the eight-sided window, against which the dining table was built. The window looked out on to a Japanese garden with a bare vine maple, three bare white birches, and a large granite boulder. A small black and white bird huddled on the bare, thin branches of the vine maple, completely exposed.

That's how I've been feeling, Beth mused, watching the bird all alone and out in the cold. But hopefully things are changing!

She turned to smile at Mom, and just as she opened her mouth to tell her about going to visit Alice Goddard, the sky cracked again. Beth swiveled around. The little bird was gone. The sky had turned black and hail thudded the roof, the trees, the ground.

"I don't believe it," Mom said as she stood by the table, looking out of the window, with her arm across Beth's shoulders. "I'm going to phone the choir director and suggest we cancel."

The wind drove through the garden, bringing more hail. Thick swirls spun past the window. While Mom phoned from the study on the opposite side of the house, Beth thought about Dad and Ted, and her stomach seized with worry about the two of them out in the storm. Suddenly an idea occurred to her, and she joined Mom in the study. Bookshelves lined the room that stuck out from the side of the house like a sore thumb. The wind bellowed and the study rattled almost as if it were getting ready to lift off. Beth felt like Dorothy on the way to the Land of Oz, and while she leafed through the thin Cedar Island phone book, she pictured Michael Jackson as the scarecrow in the movie version of *The Wiz*.

Beth turned to the S's. After Mom left the room, she stared at the black window, at the flashing streaks of hail, and held her hand on the telephone. Maybe I shouldn't call Ted, she thought. What if he's safe at home and eating dinner and doesn't want me to bug him? She ran her finger down the column and stopped at Sealley. There was only one in the book.

"Rats!" she said out loud. "I'm going to worry all night if I don't phone and find out that he got home safely. What if . . ." All kinds of horrible thoughts pressed on her. Beth wrinkled her forehead and dialed Ted's number.

Chapter Eight

Suddenly the house seemed to jump two feet, settling back with a crash.

"Are you all right?" Mom called from the other end of the house.

"Yes," Beth called, and found she was saying it into the phone which was ringing.

"Hello." A cheery voice answered. It was a voice Beth recognized from that morning at school in front of the sign-up sheet for the writing contest. Emily Summers. What's she doing at Ted's house? thought Beth. Her nerves jangled.

"Hello, hello," Emily said. "Anybody there?"

It would *have* to be Emily, thought Beth, while her stomach sank. Do I put down the telephone, or do I ask to speak to Ted, or what?

"Hi, Emily," she said quickly, before she lost her nerve and put down the phone. "It's Beth. I . . ."

"Hi, Beth," interrupted Emily. "How'd the meeting go? Could you read my writing okay?"

"Yes." And before Beth could bring up the subject of Ted, Emily continued.

"Were you able to follow what everyone was saying?"

"I scribbled pretty fast," Beth said. "I'll have to recopy what I wrote so you can read it at the next meeting."

"No prob," Emily said. "I really appreciate your doing that for me."

Then there was a pause. Beth watched the wind lashing the window, striking it with such a force that she worried that the window would break. Crack! A jagged streak of light hit the driveway, illuminating the evergreens. The window stayed intact.

"Are you okay over there?" Emily called into the phone.

Beth's voice shook. "Y-yes," she said. "But I was wondering, did Ted get home?"

Lightning whitened the sky again. Beth said, "I hope you don't mind my calling, but I was kind of worried." She listened for Emily's response, but there was no answer.

Maybe she's gone for Ted, thought Beth, feeling uneasy. It was bad enough calling Ted in the first place, but calling and reaching Emily made it one hundred times worse.

Beth waited, but there was still no answer. Then she realized with an awful shock that the telephone line was dead.

"Rats!" she muttered, crashing the phone back on the hook. I'm so stupid. I should have telephoned earlier. What if Ted *is* caught under a fallen tree? Or a broken telephone line? I let my own inferiority feelings stop me from telephoning in time, and now, if he isn't home, no one will know where he is.

And then Beth didn't care what Emily thought about her calling Ted's house. All she wanted to know was whether Ted was safe.

Oh! she thought as a light went on in her head. Emily knows I called and was asking about Ted. So she'll assume that he took me home after the meeting, and they'll look for him on the roads between my house and wherever he lives. I mean, everyone knows I live in the Kawaguchi house, right?

Reassured that at least Ted would be found if he wasn't home, Beth tried to think of something else other than the awful picture of Ted caught under a branch. But all she could think of was Emily, and how Emily flirted non-stop with Ted. How they had seemed so much alike. Both winners, she thought, and I bet Emily's the 'favorite person' he was talking about when we went to Alice Goddard's. I'm such a fool to expect someone like Ted Sealley to be interested in someone like me!

Confused and agitated, Beth wanted to scream with the wind. She pounded her fists on her hips until the feeling subsided. Then she worried again about Ted. Is he safe? Her heart raced. And what about Emily? Answering the Sealleys' telephone as if she lived there.

Suddenly the bulbs flickered, dimmed, and died. The study plunged into darkness, a deep intense blackness. The wind rattled the roof as Beth stumbled through the dark house into the kitchen, where Mom was already rummaging for candles in a drawer under the counter.

Hearing someone's feet stomping on the steps outside, Beth unlatched the door and threw her arms around Dad.

"My goodness, I'm glad to see you both," Dad exclaimed, bending over to kiss Mom while he hugged Beth.

"Is it awful out?" Beth asked, trembling, trying not to think of Ted.

The water was so rough that the candy machine on the ferry tipped over," Dad said. He took off his overcoat and draped it over a chair to dry.

"What about the roads?" Beth dreaded Dad's answer.

"Slippery," Dad said, striking a match to light the old Christmas candle Mom had set on the counter. "And a lot of fallen branches."

Beth's stomach lurched. She stared at the dark shadows cast in the glow from the thick candy-cane-striped candle as her thoughts seized on Ted. Her shoulders tightened and she barely paid attention when Mom took dinner out of the oven.

Beth shoved food back and forth on her plate, and even though it was one of her favorite dinners, she couldn't eat. Finally Beth pushed back from the table and said weakly, "I'm going to bed."

"Are you sick, sweetheart?" Dad asked.

She shook her head.

"Is school getting you down?"

Beth dropped back into her chair. She twisted the edge of her napkin and tried to find the words to tell Dad about Ted. She looked at his face in the dim light. Despite the shadows in the room, he didn't look nearly as exhausted as he used to look in Bethesda. I'm glad we moved, she thought, I know

Dad needed to get away from the city. But why did I have to get so hung up on Ted, particularly when it's obvious that Emily is the woman in his life? He's probably safe and sound at home and kissing Emily this very second. Beth knotted her fists into her stomach, then darted away from the table and over to the ladder leading to her bedroom in the loft. She climbed up, conscious that Mom and Dad were watching her from the table, and that they were worried.

Beth sunk onto her bed, wrapping her arms around her big soft pillow. She rocked back and forth. Her thoughts seemed to be whirling as fast as the storm, and she forced herself to be calm. "Relax," she whispered under her breath. "He's all right. He's all right." She chanted over and over and finally felt her muscles loosen. She kicked off her loafers and snuggled down on the bed. Her room was over the kitchen and she could hear Mom and Dad talking in the kitchen, but she couldn't make out their words.

After a few minutes, Dad climbed up the ladder to the loft. He pulled her chair away from the desk built into a small bay window, and sat on the chair backward.

"Tell me what's wrong, sweetheart."

Beth bit her bottom lip. The words wouldn't come.

"It can't be that bad, whatever it is," Dad said. "Look on the bright side."

Despite herself, Beth giggled.

"Want to share the joke?" Dad slouched down on the chair, resting his broad chin on his hands.

How can anyone look on the bright side with all the lights out and the house shaking as if it were traveling through a tunnel into the Twilight Zone, thought Beth.

"What's going on? Is there anything I can do to help?" her father asked gently.

Beth suddenly felt as if someone had pried open her mouth. She told Dad her fears about Ted's not arriving home safely.

"What time did Ted leave here?" Dad asked.

"About five."

"It doesn't take more than fifteen minutes to drive to any place on the island," Dad said kindly. "I think he would have gotten home before the storm really turned into a gale."

Beth sat up, still hugging the pillow. "Of course," she said. "How could I be so stupid?" She took a deep breath and for the first time in what seemed like hours, she felt nearly normal.

Dad didn't speak for a few minutes, and then he said, "Have you been feeling stupid a lot lately?"

"How did you guess?"

"Something about how you've been holding yourself in. Some of the things you've said. I never knew you to feel stupid before."

"I've been making the best of it at Cedar Island High," Beth blurted out, "and today was a pretty good day, but basically I'm a failure. I'm no good at anything."

"I don't understand." Dad seemed surprised.

"I don't win anything. I'm doing as Frank said, trying out for lots of things, but I always fail. I'm never good enough."

Dad swept his hands through his hair and rubbed his eyes. Then he said in a clear voice, "One way to be a success is never to try anything."

"Huh?"

"Here's another way of putting it," Dad said slowly, his face crinkling in the candlelight. "If you're afraid of failure, you'll never do anything."

"You mean, if I don't try out for things, then I'll never find out whether I'm a failure or not, and I can think of myself as successful?"

Dad grinned. "I also like to think of success as feeling good about oneself."

"How can I feel good about myself if I'm always a failure?"

"Double-talk," Dad said. "You're only a failure if you think of yourself that way."

"I *am*." Beth felt like shouting to make herself heard above the wind roaring around the house.

"If you try your hardest and don't win," Dad explained, "you still have the satisfaction of knowing that you did your best. It's how *you* do that's important, not how you do in comparison to everyone else."

"But Dad," Beth said, trying to make her father understand, "how am I going to have friends and meet people if I can't get into any of the things I try out for?''

"All you've done is find out that you've been trying out for the wrong things," Dad pointed out. "You can't stop now. You've made an excellent start. Look at all the activities you've eliminated already."

"How can you be so positive about everything?" Beth asked, not sure whether to laugh or cry at Dad's words of wisdom.

"Forty-five years gives me a bit of an edge on you," Dad said. "Plus I didn't have to move into a strange school in my junior year of high school. And I will confess that I sometimes feel a little guilty for dragging you away from your friends. . . ." His voice trailed off.

"I do like it here," Beth said. "I do, really. It's just that I'm not making much progress."

"Maybe you're expecting too much of yourself."

"Maybe," Beth said slowly.

"Be nice to that side of you that thinks you're stupid."

Beth grimaced. She certainly didn't want to be nice to *that* part of herself.

"I've been thinking of something," Dad said. "A present for Easter, and I want your opinion on it."

"For Mom?"

"For all of us. Shall we send Frank a plane ticket to come out during his spring break and spend Easter with us?"

"Great!" Beth clapped her hands and immediately felt more peaceful. Frank always had ideas to help her hang in there and make a go of everything.

"As soon as the phone lines are fixed, we'll call him and see if he has time to come out."

Mom climbed up the ladder. She kissed Beth on the cheek, and then said, "Everything okay?"

"Much better, thanks," Beth said. "But now I'm exhausted."

Dad replaced the desk chair, and for a moment both Mom and Dad smiled down at her before they lowered themselves down the ladder into the main room. After they left, it was all Beth could do to put on her pajamas and tuck herself into bed.

Chapter Nine

Beth was riding across the United States in a yellow school bus. The bus was full of kids, but when she looked around, she saw, with a dreadful sinking feeling, that she didn't know any of them. She sat alone in the back seat, biting her nails.

Suddenly a hairy monster jumped onto the rear bumper, slowing the bus. The bus driver paid no attention. "I'll get you," the monster growled as he reached toward the window with long, sharp claws. The glass shattered and Beth screamed, waking up from her nightmare.

Outside the storm raged on. "A dream," she whispered. "It's only a dream."

Finally she fell asleep again and next thing she knew, Dad was standing on her ladder, poking his head into the loft, and saying, "No school today!"

Beth sat up. "How do you know?"

"I heard the announcement on Frank's Coke can."

Beth smiled. She knew her father was referring to Frank's transistor radio, the one that looked just like a Coke can. As Dad climbed down the ladder, Beth curled back under the covers. She listened hard, but did not hear anything. Not the storm. Not the pump bringing water up from the well. Not Luther, the neighbor's rooster, crowing his usual morning greeting. It was ominously silent, as if the tumult from the night before had stopped the world.

Oh, rats! thought Beth, throwing back the covers and leaping out of bed into the damp cold room. Now I don't get to see Ted, or find out if he's okay.

Beth pulled on jeans, a wool sweater, a thick navy cardigan, and a pair of woolen socks that Frank had outgrown, and then climbed downstairs. Mom and Dad sat at the teak table with their coats and scarves on. The house was freezing cold.

Outside, the yard was littered with scraps of tar paper that had blown off their decaying shed's old roof. Evergreen branches covered the ground and bundles of gritty snow lay in windswept drifts.

"No electricity yet?" Beth said through chattering teeth, although the answer was obvious.

"None," Dad said, "and no telephone, either. And without electricity, we can't operate the pump for our water."

"Oh!" Beth said, jerking up her head. "Now I know what Alice Goddard meant about getting water."

"We still have a lot to learn about living on this island," Dad said, grinning up at Beth. "I suggest we drive into the village and see if we can get breakfast at The Dew Drop Inn. I desperately need a hot cup of coffee."

"I bet they don't have electricity, either," Mom said.

"Or heat," Beth said.

"We won't know until we get there," Dad commented optimistically.

Beth grinned at Dad's typically positive remark. I wish I could be more like him, she thought as she reached for her down jacket in the closet. I've got to stop being so stupid.

Then she remembered her dream. Was the monster only a part of herself that wanted to be recognized rather than ignored?

Beth wound a navy and white scarf around her head, and said cheerfully, "I'm up for it."

"Me, too," Mom said, shivering. "And the first remodeling we've got to do to this house, David, is put a wood stove in the kitchen."

While Dad drove their Toyota wagon to the village, Beth told her parents about Alice Goddard and her Monarch stove, sheep, and honey.

"I bet she's got some interesting old stories to tell about the island," Dad said. "She might give you some ideas for the writing contest.

But Beth was already pushing some ideas around in her own mind. She wanted to write something about the monster, and about success and failure, and about feeling colossally stupid.

The Toyota skidded several times on the slick roads, and everyone held their breath until they reached the old house near the ferry terminal. The house had been converted into a restaurant called The Dew Drop Inn. It had high-backed wooden booths along one side of what must have been a large elegant living room at one time. A log fire blazed in the tile fireplace at the far end, immediately warming Beth and her parents.

"It's like the fifties again, isn't it," Mom said after they sat down in the only empty booth. Pictures of Elvis Presley hung on the walls. A bright red and yellow juke box stood near the windows, silent, of course, for there was no electricity in the village, either.

"Reminds me of our first date," Dad said, winking at Mom. She kissed the tips of her fingers and blew him a kiss. Beth was glad the backs of the booth were high so that no one could see them carrying on like two teenagers, instead of respectable parents.

A waitress wearing black wool slacks and a red vest over a full-sleeved white blouse came to their booth. "All we can offer you is hot porridge with maple syrup and cream," she said apologetically.

"And coffee?" Dad asked in a plaintive voice.

"And coffee," the waitress confirmed with a friendly grin.

"I'd love some porridge," Mom said.

"Me, too," Beth added.

"And a big bowl for the daddy bear," Dad concluded, grinning.

The waitress smiled and left for the kitchen in the back room. She returned immediately with three white ceramic mugs of steaming black coffee. Beth poured cream into hers, stirred in a heaping teaspoon of sugar, and began to sip it slowly. The waitress returned with three bowls of hot oatmeal cereal and a jug of maple syrup, and everyone dug in hungrily.

"More cereal?" the waitress asked after they had finished.

"It was yummy," Beth said, "but I've had enough."

"Next time you come, we'll have the regular menu," said the waitress, pouring more coffee for everyone. "But this was the best we could do today, under the circumstances."

"Were there any accidents during the storm?" blurted Beth. She couldn't get rid of the worry that something had happened to Ted.

"I'm sure we would have heard if there was," the waitress said. "Doc Milt was in here a bit ago, and he said it was the first storm he'd been able to sleep through without having to care for someone caught under a fallen tree."

"Thank heaven," Beth's mom said.

Beth breathed a sigh of relief, then worried again. Maybe Ted had been caught under a tree but no one had found him. I have to know how he is, she thought. I can't wait another day to find out.

After her father paid the bill, he put his arm across Beth's back and said, "Let's go and check on your friend."

"I don't know where he lives," Beth said, feeling the color drain from her face.

"Can we check the telephone book for his address?"

"Only box numbers are listed," Beth said shortly, thinking how absentminded her father was for not remembering that Cedar Island didn't have street addresses.

"Will the waitress know?" he asked.

"Probably," Beth said. "Everyone on the island seems to know where everyone else lives."

"Do you want to ask her?"

Beth struggled with her dad's suggestion. She had to know how Ted was, but what if he and Emily were going together? They'd probably spent a lot of time at the Dew Drop and the waitress might think it was odd that Beth was so concerned.

As her parents went out the door, the urge to know that Ted was safe at home pushed Beth forward. Sure enough, the waitress knew exactly where the Sealleys lived. She drew a map on a paper napkin.

"Thanks," Beth said, feeling relieved that the waitress didn't seem at all interested in whether she was going to visit Ted or not. She left the building and joined her mom and dad in the Toyota.

Mr. Hamilton drove down the north side of the island, arriving at Ted's place in half an hour, longer than they would have taken under ordinary circumstances because they had to detour around dead branches littering the roads.

An old ringer washer, outfitted with a mailbox, stood at the entrance to their drive. Painted across the tub, in rainbow letters, was SEALLEY.

"We've got the right place," Beth said, and Dad turned in. They hadn't gone more than fifty feet before the road turned sharply. Ahead of them stood an ultramodern cedar house against a backdrop of sky and water. The office buildings of Seattle faded into the far distance with just the faintest outline of the Cascade Mountains behind them. Ted's car was parked to one side of the house.

"He's fine," Beth said quickly. "We can back out."

Her father continued to go down the driveway.

"Back up," Beth hissed in a sharp voice. "Don't go any farther. That's Ted's car so I know he got home safe. Please don't go down."

But by the time she finished talking, Dad had already driven to the end of the driveway. He stopped the car and turned around to look at Beth. "Are you feeling shy?" he asked kindly.

"I don't want Ted to see me, Dad," Beth whispered, feeling as if she would die of embarrassment if Ted appeared at that moment. "I just wanted to know if he had gotten home okay. Please turn around."

Before Dad could start the car again, Ted Sealley's tall, lean figure appeared at the doorway of a flat-roofed building that was separate from the main house. Beth's first impulse was to duck under the car seat, but she saw that Ted had recognized her and was running over. Oh, rats! she thought. What do I do now?

"Hi." Beth opened the car door, almost losing her loafers in her hurry to get out. "Sorry to bother you, but I was worried. I just had to know that you had gotten home safely in that storm."

Ted's high cheekbones were flushed. He grinned and said, "Emily told me you phoned and the line went dead. I didn't know whether lightning had struck your house or not. I was going to phone you as soon as we got connected again."

Beth lifted up her shoulders and relaxed them again. She looked past Ted and up at the sky. A few streamers of sunshine poked through overhanging clouds, seeming to wind them into balls.

"It's gorgeous," said Beth, feeling breathless. "We never had days like this back in Maryland."

"The sunshine after the storm," said Ted. "It almost makes it worth while, except that my dad's fussing because he can't get going on his latest invention without being able to use his power tools."

Ted had barely finished saying "power" when the bulb in a ships' lantern hanging on the corner of the house beamed on. Ted snapped his fingers and said, "See! I can do magic!"

Beth laughed.

"Watch," said Ted, snapping his fingers again. The front door of the house immediately opened. A tall man with hair almost as blond as Ted's hurried out.

"That's my dad," Ted said. "He can't wait to get into his workshop, which is that little building you see here." He pointed toward the flat-roofed building next to the house.

"Well," Ted's father said as he approached the Toyota, "you've brought both the electricity and the sunshine. Welcome!"

Beth's mom and dad opened the car door and got out.

"I'm David Hamilton," said Beth's dad, holding out his hand. "Pleased to meet you."

How does Dad do it? thought Beth. He's never shy about introducing himself. I wish I could say the same for myself.

After all introductions were made, Sam Sealley, Ted's father, said, "Please come in. Now that we have all the modern conveniences, like electricity, I can offer you some hospitality.''

Beth started to follow them, but Ted silently motioned for Beth to follow him around the side of the house. He pointed southeast across the water. Standing majestically, as if suspended from the sky, was Mount Rainier. It looked like a giant ice cream cone painted on a massive blue billboard.

Ted stretched both arms wide as if to reach for this ice cream cone. ''I always believe that when Mt. Rainier's visible, it's an omen that something wonderful is going to happen,'' he explained. ''And there the mountain is, and here you are!''

Beth beamed, then gazed back across the broad expanse of rolling water at the mountain. A white ferry chugged toward Seattle. She sniffed, smelling salt water mingled with wood smoke, which was coming from the large stone chimney.

''The weather's changed so fast,'' she said. ''It doesn't seem like the same place it was yesterday.'' And my life has changed so fast, she thought, I don't feel like the same person I was yesterday.

''Welcome to the Pacific Northwest,'' Ted said, and for the first time since Christmas, Beth actually felt as if she were glad to be on Cedar Island. ''But come on into the house,'' Ted continued. ''Emily and my sister Margot are probably making hot chocolate.''

''Emily?'' Beth couldn't help it; the name popped out like a frog jumping from a creek. She wished she could turn around and drive away without another word. For her, the whole day was spoiled.

Chapter Ten

I don't want to go into that house and face Emily, thought Beth as they walked along the gravel path circling the house. I wish I had the nerve to say "No thanks," and go sit by myself in the car.

"Mom's greenhouse," Ted explained when they turned at sharp angles to circumvent a glassed extension of the house. "She loved to lie in here when she was sick. She used to say that she could hear the plants talking."

"I wish I could have known your mom," Beth said quietly.

"I wish you could have, too," Ted said. "You're like her in some ways. She seemed to be aloof with people, too, but she didn't really mean to be. It was just that she was shy and never liked to meet strangers."

"I never thought of myself as being aloof," Beth said slowly. "I just have a hard time getting to know people."

"My mom used to say that, too," Ted said. He put his hand on her back and directed her across the cobble-stone patio leading to the front door of the house. Beth breathed deeply with the pleasure of his hand against her back, and decided suddenly, what the heck, I'll go into the house even if Emily is there making cocoa in Ted's kitchen.

A stained-glass window covered the top third of the front door. It was a deep rich blue, with a nautilus shape filled with etched white glass in the center piece.

Tracing the curves of the shell with her finger, Beth said, "It's exquisite."

"My mom made it," Ted said. "She used to do a lot of stained glass windows for people on the island."

Beth detected a heaviness settle over him as he opened the front door. She wanted to hold his hand, but she heard Mr. Sealley talking to Mom and Dad on the right side of the hall, and she heard Emily's loud, cheery voice from the left side, so she tucked her hand into her jacket pocket instead. Beth followed Ted through a wide hall toward the rear of the house. The hall's floor was the same pebbled concrete as the patio, and the walls were hung with paintings.

"Margot did that," Ted said when Beth stopped to look at a painting of an eagle holding a salmon in its claws.

The kitchen filled one wing of the house, and Emily, sure enough, was standing beside the stove. Emily looked smashing in a mauve ski outfit. Her legs were long and, even in the padded pants, looked as thin as the legs of a *Vogue* model.

Beth forced herself to say hello, and to act as if she couldn't care less whether Emily was in Ted's house or not.

"I'm sorry I forgot to return your pencil," Beth said after they exchanged comments about the weather.

"That's okay," Emily said. "My pop flies for United and we've got loads. They're promotional pencils."

"Next time you fly, just remember who to fly with," Ted said jokingly. He tweaked Emily's cheek.

"Hey, fly-boy," retorted Emily, flicking a dishtowel at his legs. "You've got flying feet, so you don't need an airplane."

Beth moved toward the window. She could almost feel herself turning green, and couldn't stand to see how they teased each other.

The enormous kitchen window faced Seattle, which shimmered on the other side of the water. Pink geraniums grew in a long cedar box in front of the window. Margot, Ted's fourteen-year-old sister, came into the kitchen with a watering can, and as she poured water over the geraniums, she said to Beth, "Hi, how's everything with you?"

"Fine," Beth lied.

"Yeah, me, too," said Margot in a droopy voice.

Beth looked at her and they suddenly both grinned.

Margot was blonde, like Ted and their father, and had green eyes, too. But unlike Ted, she was chubby and had plump cheeks. She also had a cute way of tilting her head sideways, like a bird cocking its head to listen to the world.

"At least we don't have to drag ourselves to that school," said Margot.

"Don't you like Cedar Island High?" Beth asked, startled at Margot's words.

"Does anybody?"

"Sure they do," Emily called from the stove where she and Ted were mixing hot milk with cocoa powder into mugs. "I love it there."

"Oh, her!" said Margot, jerking her thumb in Emily's direction. "She thinks this island is the center of the universe."

It's because she's got Ted, thought Beth. That's why Emily likes school so much. I would, too, if . . . if only . . . She couldn't bear to finish the thought.

"I want to go back east to the North Carolina School of the Arts," said Margot, "but Dad won't let me."

"Where won't I let you go?" Margot's dad had completed a tour of the house with Beth's parents. Beth wished she had gone with them, instead of having to stay in the kitchen and watch Emily and Ted carry on.

"Same old story," said Ted. He came to the window with two mugs of hot chocolate. Handing one to Beth, he said, "Margot can't stop talking about going away to boarding school. I think she just wants to get out of taking her turn with the dinners and housework."

"Nonsense," said Margot, holding out her hand. "Where's my hot chocolate?"

"I'm not your servant," said Ted, grinning when Margot stuck out her tongue.

Emily joined them at the window with two more mugs and said, "Here, pip-squeak."

Sam Sealley poured cocoa for himself and the Hamiltons, who were sitting at the kitchen table. It was a large round table of glass, with a wrought-iron base. Leaded into the center of the glass was a large parrot with bright red, blue, and yellow feathers.

Another of Ted's mother's creations, thought Beth. She sipped the rich chocolate and thought, How awful it must have been for them. No wonder Mr. Sealley doesn't want Margot to go away. But it's no wonder that she wants to leave this house with all its reminders of her mother.

"Penny for your thoughts," said Ted, looking down at her.

"Cliché!" Emily sounded as if she were calling Bingo.

"Hold your horses, Emily Summers," retorted Ted. "I'm not talking to you, I'm talking to Beth."

"Just listen to him," Emily said to no one in particular. "All he can do is speak in clichés. Did you fail Mrs. Atkinson's English by any chance?" Her voice became high and squeaky as she taunted Ted.

Beth wished she could sink out of sight. She hated watching Emily's games, even though she was glad she didn't have to tell Ted what she was thinking, or try to make something up.

"Just 'cause you're such a hotshot in English doesn't mean you can knock the rest of us down," Ted said, bumping his hip against Emily's.

Beth was overjoyed when Mom, at that moment, put down her mug and said, "We must be going."

She must have read my mind, thought Beth as they said good-bye and walked out to their Toyota. As Dad turned the car around to leave, she tried to smile. But it was all she could do to wave at Ted, Emily, and Margot standing together in the driveway.

Ted and Emily were obviously made for each other. They even looked a little bit alike. Beth gritted her teeth when she painfully remembered how they kidded each other, made funny faces, and generally never left each other alone. She was obviously a total idiot to think that someone like Ted Sealley would go for someone who never knew what to say, who daydreamed too much, who was plain-looking, and who gave everyone the feeling that she was aloof. Obviously he had a good thing going with green-eyed, blond-haired, flip and friendly Emily Summers. Why would he want to break that off?

Some of Ted's comments drifted into her negative thoughts, and she wondered, in spite of herself, what he had meant. He shouldn't say he's glad to see me, she thought at last, he's just putting me on. He must not realize how crazy I am about him, and how totally impossible it is for us to be "just friends." I can't. I'd rather have nothing to do with Ted than have to watch him and Emily cooing at each other like silly lovebirds.

Not exactly lovebirds, she decided when Dad drove toward their house. But exactly like two people who feel very comfortable together. Otherwise why would Emily always be at his house? And why would they talk to each other like they do?

Something didn't quite add up, but Beth, for the life of her, couldn't figure out what it was. She suddenly felt totally and absolutely lonely and confused. It was as if the big hairy monster of her dream was tightening his grip on her shoulder and there was nothing she could do about it. Nothing at all!

Chapter Eleven

Beth was back to school on Thursday. After she had hung her down jacket in her locker, she turned around, and there was Ted. He wore a white button-down shirt, brown cords, and a Killer Whale button in support of Greenpeace on his brown V-neck sweater.

"Hi," he said. "How are you?"

"Fine, thanks," Beth said as her mind blanked out. She could think of nothing else to say.

Why is it, she thought as they walked down the hall, that the minute I see Ted I go into orbit?

Her heart thumped so much she thought he must hear it and think her weird. She took several deep breaths and tried to relax.

"Did your power ever come on?" Ted asked after they passed the principal's office.

"Yes," Beth said.

"Good." Ted switched his books to his other arm and continued walking.

Since Beth was going in the same direction, she continued beside him, feeling more and more like a fool. What if Emily sees me? she thought. I'll be in for it! What *it* was, she wasn't quite sure, but she was sure she didn't want to tangle with Emily over Ted.

"See you," Ted said when they parted at the end of the main hall.

"See you," responded Beth, wondering if she'd ever see him again after her inability to talk to him. Why couldn't she be flippant like Emily, and say the first thing that came into her head. But then again, nothing ever came into her head. Nothing she wanted to share with anyone else, that is!

Beth hurried into Chemistry lab. Eggie walked over to her stool and said, "Everything's set for the Fifties Dance."

"Great," Beth said, trying to get some enthusiasm into her voice.

"Yep," said Eggie. "My father's dance band will play for the pleasure of playing. In other words, it won't cost the ASB a penny."

"Sounds like fun," Beth said although she saw no fun in it for her. Ted was going with Emily, that was a foregone conclusion, and she might as well accept the fact right now.

"My dad's looking for a female vocalist," continued Eggie. "You don't happen to know anyone who sings a lot of fifties songs, would you?"

"My mom," Beth suggested, shrugging her shoulders.

"Fantastic," Eggie said. "Do you think my dad could call her and talk to her?"

"Sure."

"Your last name's Hamilton, right?"

"Yes," Beth said, "but we're not in the new phone book yet." She ripped a piece of paper from her looseleaf book and wrote down the number. "Here. Tell your dad that Mom will be out tonight. She goes to choir practice at Island Church."

"That's even better," Eggie said, swinging his briefcase. "My dad'll probably stop by the church and talk to her in person. He's anxious to find a singer before the dance."

When the bell rang, Beth got down to work. She pushed thoughts of Ted and the dance out of her head whenever they popped in, which was at least once every five minutes. If I don't start concentrating, I'm going to fail Chemistry, she thought, frowning over the microscope. Taking a deep breath, she was finally able to pay attention.

In English Lit, Mrs. Atkinson spoke to her during the last fifteen-minute extempt writing time, an exercise in which

they were to write their thoughts continuously, without re-
gard to meaning, form, or punctuation.

"Have you chosen a topic for your writing entry, Beth?"
Mrs. Atkinson leaned over Beth's desk and spoke quietly,
her breath smelling of cinnamon. Everything about this
teacher looked quiet: plain brown hair, plain white blouse,
plain wool skirt, sensible shoes with soft soles that wouldn't
make a noise, eyes . . .

Beth retracted that quiet image when she looked deeply
into Mrs. Atkinson's eyes. They were intense brown eyes
that looked as if they contained thoughts only the thickest
book of philosophy might reveal.

"I don't know what I'm going to write about," Beth said,
still looking into Mrs. Atkinson's eyes. "I've been thinking,
but haven't decided."

"Write about something you know the most about," Mrs.
Atkinson said in her soft voice.

Beth wiped her hands on her jeans. "I don't know much
about anything," she said.

"Do you know anything about yourself?"

Sure, thought Beth. I know I'm stupid.

Mrs. Atkinson looked at a thin silver watch on her arm and
clapped her hands to indicate the end of the extempt writing
time. While she was waiting for everyone to put down their
pens, she said, "Writing should be as easy as speaking.
Don't make it difficult for yourself."

As easy as speaking? I can't speak, thought Beth, and I
can't write either. I don't know what I'm doing entering a
writing contest, even if it did, sort of, help me meet Ted
Sealley!

At lunch, Beth sat at the corner table with Rosie, as usual.
When Emily Summers came by carrying a tray, she said,
"Mind if I sit down?"

"Join the club," Rosie said as she unwrapped her Milky
Way bar. "We aren't exclusive."

Today Emily wore a mauve jumpsuit with a black silk scarf
tied in a triangle over her slim hips. Black disks dangled from
her ears. In comparison, Beth felt dumpy and old-fashioned

in her jeans and sweater.

"I can leave," Emily said in a funny voice, "if this is a private conversation."

"Knock it off, Emily," Rosie said. "You know I'm only teasing."

Emily plopped down into the chair and opened her lunch sack. She took out two peanut-butter-and-jam sandwiches, a bag of tortilla chips, a Midnight Mint cookie, a can of V-8 juice, and a carrot.

"Wow," Beth blurted, staring at Emily's mammoth lunch. "I'd be a tub if I ate that much."

"They used to call me pencil in grade school because I was so thin," Emily said as she unwrapped one of her sandwiches. "That's why I started giving away pencils. Everytime anyone lost or forgot a pencil, I had an extra one. It didn't cost me any money, but it sure enhanced my image. It wasn't long before everyone forgot that they called me 'Pencil' because I was so skinny, and called me that because I handed out free pencils."

Beth grinned at Emily, and although she hadn't been that pleased to have her sit at the table, she could sympathize with her feelings about wanting to improve her image.

"I guess I forgot your pencil again," Beth said, rummaging in her purse. "I must have left it on my desk at home."

"Forget it," Emily said. "As I said, I have boxes of them."

"You sound like an old outboard engine with all that chewing," growled a male voice behind them. Beth looked around and and saw Rosie's boyfriend, Jens.

Jens had graduated from Cedar Island High two years ago. He was stocky and very rugged. He looked like he could heave fish around a rolling ship's deck—which was what he did six months of the year, working on his uncle's fishing boat in Alaska.

"Where'd my sweetie go?" Jens asked.

"I bet she's gone for another Milky Way," said Emily.

Sure enough, Rosie appeared with another chocolate bar. She threw her arms around Jens and after a quick hug, said in her perky way, "What's up?"

"I've gotta go to Seattle for engine parts," Jens said. "I figured I'd come early and join you for lunch."

"Lunch?" Emily said. "All Rosie eats is candy bars."

"Want a bite?" asked Rosie, holding her bar to Jens's mouth.

"You don't eat properly," Jens said. "How can you compete in track if you don't eat good food."

"Chocolate is good food," said Rosie, taking a big bite of her bar.

"It is not," Jens insisted, and Beth got the distinct feeling that he could be very stubborn when he wanted to be.

Rosie closed one eye and jutted her small round chin toward Jens. Her eyes glinted and the message was clear. Rosie ate what she wanted!

"Come to the Dew Drop Friday night," Rosie said, turning to Emily. "All profits that night go to buy new track suits."

"Darn!" Emily said. "A party, and I can't go."

"Why not?" Rosie asked and she tossed her ponytail.

"Pop's coming home that night," Emily said excitedly.

Why's she so hung up on staying home to see her father? thought Beth.

"Do you want me to try and squeeze a notice into the paper?" Emily asked.

"I meant to let you know sooner, so you could get us some free publicity," Rosie said. "But I got distracted by the storm, and forgot to phone."

You couldn't have reached Emily anyway, thought Beth, remembering that Emily was over at Ted's. Unable to eat, Beth rewrapped her sandwich.

"You'll come to the benefit with Jens and me, won't you, Beth?"

"Maybe." Beth didn't dare tell Rosie that the only reason she would go was because Emily was not going, and it meant Ted would be alone!

"I'm surprised Ted hasn't said anything to me," Emily said.

"I am, too," Rosie said, and Beth looked at her, unwilling to believe that Rosie knew about Ted and Emily all along and hadn't said a word about their relationship to her. "We've been planning it for two weeks. Ted ought to have told you, especially since we arranged it at the Dew Drop together."

Beth watched Emily drinking her V-8 juice. She behaved as if there were no bad vibrations between them, and Beth tried to stop her hateful feelings toward Emily. But there was no escaping the fact, despite Emily's friendliness, Beth couldn't be comfortable with her. Not until she knew for certain what was going on between Emily and Ted.

"Ted's gone to see the principal about the May Day Dance," Emily said, breaking into Beth's reveries. "Lucky for us, our principal thinks we should have more parties, rather than less, since there's no place to go on this rock for a good time."

Good Time Girl, thought Beth. That's all Emily is, despite what she told me about the pencils. I don't have to be jealous of someone like her. But Beth had to admit that just because she decided she didn't have to be jealous of someone like Emily, didn't mean she wasn't.

"I'm so bored with Cedar Island," continued Emily. "I'm going to split as soon as we graduate."

This is a real switch. I thought she loved it here, thought Beth. Maybe Emily and Ted had a fight.

Rosie, Jens, and Emily talked on about the Fifties Dance but Beth got hung up on the thought that *if* Ted had wanted to invite her to the dance, he would have done so when he drove her home after the meeting.

Emily passed her some tortilla chips, but Beth declined. Just being next to Emily was poison, although . . . a part of her mind stopped. If it hadn't been for Emily, Beth realized, I wouldn't have gotten to know Ted as well as I have. And knowing him is better than nothing. Or is it?

"By the way," Emily said just as they were getting ready to leave the lunchroom, "can you come to Mrs. Atkinson's after school and help us lay out the paper? It'd be fabulous if you would. I can get you a ride home. Don't worry about missing the school bus."

"Okay," Beth said, but for the remainder of the afternoon she wondered what on earth possessed her to say yes. The less time she spent with Emily Summers, the better!

Chapter Twelve

"I've got orders to drive you home," Ted said after the bell rang at the end of Algebra. He tapped his foot on the floor. Beth, looking down, noticed a capital R on his right shoe.

Oh, great! she thought. Emily's put Ted up to taking me home after I work on the paper for her. We'll make a happy little threesome in the Plymouth.

"I've got track practice," Ted said as they walked down the hall, "so if you finish before I do, come out to the field. Otherwise I'll come to Mrs. Atkinson's room."

"You don't have to take me home if you don't want to," Beth said. "I can ask my mom to come and get me."

"I want to," Ted said, and Beth noticed a funny expression on his face.

"See you later, then," she said, and stopped at the front office to telephone Mom that she would be late.

Beth paused with her hand on the phone and realized that she was shaking. She wanted so much to go home with Ted, but not if she had to share the car with Emily.

Beth dialed and the phone rang at least ten times before Mom finally answered.

"Hello," Mom said, breathless.

"Hi," Beth said. "Where were you?"

"I've been outside cleaning up after the storm," said Mom. "What's up?"

"I'm going to be home late," Beth said. "But don't worry. I've got a ride."

"Bring your chauffeur in," Mom said. "I'd like to meet him."

"Them," corrected Beth. "And you already met them yesterday."

"Ted and Emily?" Mom said it as if those two names automatically went together.

"Yes." Beth said good-bye and hung up the phone. She dragged herself down to Mrs. Atkinson's room, thinking, What have I let myself in for? I'd rather be home helping Mom clean up the yard, than having to deal with someone as gorgeous and capable as Emily Summers.

"Hiya!" Emily called from the front of the room as Beth opened the door. "Grab a pair of scissors and I'll show you how we set up the paper."

Phillip Predo, whom Beth knew from Algebra, sat at the end of the long table underneath the windows. He held a rapidograph pen in one hand and a wadded ball of paper in the other.

He tossed the ball at Emily. She picked it up, and after uncreasing the crinkles, held the paper in front of Beth, and said, "What do you think?"

Phillip had drawn a cartoon with a group of students sitting around a single candle flame. They held slates and chalk, but wore high-fashion clothes. The teacher, who looked a little like Mrs. Atkinson, was saying, "Write a story about the good old days when we had electricity and telephones. Describe it as if you had actually been there."

Beth laughed. "I like it," she said, smoothing the paper on the table in front of Phillip.

"You think everyone will get it?" Phillip tipped his black beret onto the back of his head as he tipped back his chair to talk to Beth.

"Tough luck to those who don't," called Emily from across the room. "We're printing it, so get the final copy ready."

Phillip continued to look at Beth.

"Do it!" Emily said in an imperious voice.

"Will everyone get it?" Phillip repeated.

"You can't worry about pleasing everyone," said Beth, hoping to reassure him.

"Do you really like it?" Phillip clanged his chair back onto all four legs.

"Yes."

Phillip picked up his pen and starting drawing, and Beth wondered why her opinion seemed to matter so much. A lot I know about cartooning, she thought.

Beth moved to the end of table windows where two girls were cutting and pasting articles onto a master sheet.

"Hi," said a girl with long blond hair, "I'm Kit. I met you in the ASB meeting. Lisa"—she turned to her partner, who was wearing a powerfully scented lei—"meet Beth Hamilton."

"Hello," Lisa said. "Are you the new girl?"

"I suppose so," Beth said, hating that expression. To change the subject quickly, she said, "I like your flowers. Where'd you get them?"

"My folks just got back yesterday from Hawaii. Their plane was delayed a day because of the storm."

"My cousins are thinking of going to Hawaii for Easter," Emily said. "I might go over, too, since I can get there free."

"You're so lucky. I wish my father worked for an airline," Lisa said.

"That's what I'm going to be when I grow up," Phillip said.

"I thought you were going to be a famous cartoonist," said Emily, walking over to him and peering down at his paper.

"I'll be a pilot while I'm waiting to break into print," said Phillip. "Hey! That's gives me another idea for a cartoon."

Quickly he began doodling on a fresh sheet of paper.

Emily jabbed her finger on the crinkled original cartoon, and said in a stern voice, "Focus, Phillip. I need this by five o'clock." She looked at Beth and swept her hands up through her hair, saying, "The hassles of being an editor. It's like pulling teeth to get Phillip to follow through on one good idea before he's doodling a million more.''

Pulling teeth is a cliché, Beth wanted to say, remembering how Emily had criticized Ted for the expressions he used. But instead, Beth bit her bottom lip concentrating on fitting the articles on the master sheet in order.

The time went quickly, and at five, when she looked up, there was Ted coming through the door. His lean cheeks were flushed, and he seemed to glow. Rats, thought Beth. Why does he always have to look totally terrific?

''Ready?'' Ted asked, looking at Beth, but not Emily.

''Yes.'' Beth stretched her back, easing the strain of having bent over the table for so long.

Emily tucked all the papers in a brown manila envelope. ''Time's up, Phillip,'' she said, and when he handed her the cartoon, she tucked it into the envelope without looking.

Phillip pushed his beret over his forehead and, with a casual wave, sauntered out of the room.

''Let's go,'' Emily said, and they walked out to the Plymouth.

Should I go with them? thought Beth. I can telephone Mom to come and pick me up. Who wants to share a ride with Ted and Emily? Not me!

Just as they reached the pavement, Emily stopped. ''I forgot to call the print shop and tell them we were coming. I'll only be a minute.'' She shoved her books at Ted and hurried back to school, noisily clonking her wooden clogs across the pavement.

Where do I sit? thought Beth, but Ted solved the problem by opening the front door on the passenger side. It would be a little ridiculous to climb into the back seat now, and she was grateful that she didn't have to. And if Emily also gets into the front, she considered, I'll be able to sit next to Ted. With this thought, Beth felt a slight flush in her cheeks, and she put her hands on her face, pretending to rub her eyes.

''How was track practice?'' she asked when Ted got in on his side.

''Good,'' Ted said, smiling at her, ''but not great. I really notice it when I miss a day of training, as I did yesterday.''

"Rosie was telling me that she's been having trouble with her ankles," Beth said. "Do you have problems like that, too?"

"My only problem's my head," laughed Ted, and he banged the palm of his hand against the top of his head.

"I can relate to that," said Beth, thinking how his green eyes lit up when he laughed, and how cute he looked.

"If I can only keep my concentration, I'm fine," Ted said, "but sometimes I get to thinking about other things, and I lose it."

"You and me both," said Beth, but privately she wondered, What does he mean? Why is he looking at me in such an odd way? Before she had a chance to continue the conversation, Emily arrived and—rats—climbed into the back seat.

"We gotta hurry," she said. "The paper will go to press tonight if we get there by six. Otherwise we'll have to wait until Monday and we won't get the notice of the track benefit out to the school."

Ted spun the Plymouth out of the parking lot. Beth wanted to say, Take me home afterward, but kept her mouth shut. It was probably easier for them to drop her off first, rather than have to drive all the way back down the island after they'd gone to the print shop. Besides, she thought, they probably want more time alone.

When Ted drove around the arbutus tree in the driveway, Mom was standing on the porch in her striped overalls and blue bandanna scarf tied around her hair, looking twenty-five years old instead of forty. As she saw the car approach the house, she waved.

"I've always loved this property," said Emily, "and the crazy imaginative way Mr. Kawaguchi built this house."

"Come on over and see it anytime," said Beth, and then bit her lip. What was she saying?

"Sorry we can't stay," said Ted, gunning the engine. "We'll see you tomorrow. Say hi to your mom."

Beth jumped out. She walked up to Mom standing on the porch and thought about the way Ted had said "we." It sounded comfortable, as if he had been saying that about Emily and himself all his life.

"They're in a hurry to get out to the print shop," said Beth, hoping her voice didn't sound too hurt by the fact that Emily and Ted had dropped her off first. "They couldn't stay. Ted says hi."

"I understand." Mom kissed Beth on the cheek and said, "I've just got a few more things to do in the garden and then I'll be in."

I'm glad Mom understands, thought Beth grumpily as she walked into the house alone. I'm not sure I do!

But, she decided as she climbed up the ladder to her bedroom in the loft, I'm too strung out thinking about Ted Sealley, and I'm not going to think about him anymore.

And that, she thought as she dumped her books onto her desk, is decidedly *that!*

Chapter Thirteen

"Don't forget the benefit for the track team tonight," Rosie reminded Beth at lunch on Friday.

"Yeah," said Beth, dying to find out from Rosie what the real situation was between Emily and Ted.

"Are you coming?" asked Rosie.

Perfect opportunity to catch Ted without Emily, thought Beth, yet as much as she wanted to go, she couldn't force herself to say yes.

"Come on, come with us. We're looking forward to having you come," Rosie insisted. "We get tired of talking to each other all the time."

"I don't know," Beth hedged, feeling a leaden mass in her stomach.

"You promised," Rosie said.

"I did?" Beth studied her friend's face. "I don't remember promising."

Rosie swung her ponytail down over her forehead and back down her neck.

That did it. Beth Ann Hamilton always kept her promises, and whether she wanted to or not, she would go to The Dew Drop Inn in order to help out the Cedar Island Track Team and please her new friend Rosie McNeil.

"Maybe they'll have a benefit for the writing contest," Beth said after she finished her cheese sandwich. "Give the

winner a prize.'' And a booby prize, she thought, so I can win
something.

"They should," said Rosie. "They only send one person a
year and there are lots of good writers in this school. They
should come up with the funds to send two, at least."

"Where do they send them?" Beth asked, surprised. She
hadn't heard about this aspect of the contest.

"Some sort of summer workshop sponsored by the University of Washington," Rosie said. "I've heard Emily talking about it. She's dying to go."

"She probably will," said Beth, remembering that Emily
had said she wasn't programming herself to lose.

After Algebra, Ted asked, "Are you going to be working
on the paper again? I can drive you home after track practice."

"No," said Beth. "You took the paper up to the printer
yesterday, remember?"

Rolling his eyes, Ted banged the side of his head with the
flat of his hand. "And it's waiting in the hall right now for us
to take home and read."

"Right," said Beth, laughing up at him.

"You're not the only daydreamer in the crowd," Ted said,
patting Beth's shoulder.

Beth felt tingly all over. She was happy she'd taken more
time with her appearance that morning. She was wearing a
tartan skirt, nylons, her loafers, and a loosely knit moss-
green sweater over a white turtleneck. Her black hair was
combed neatly over her ears, and she had trimmed her bangs
an inch before dashing for the school bus that morning.

"I'd offer you a ride home," said Ted, "but I've got track
practice and Coach said if I got there early, he'd give me
some extra tips on starting."

"Thanks anyway," Beth said. "And good luck with the
workout."

"See you tomorrow," said Ted.

"See you," said Beth, feeling crushed. Ted didn't say
anything about seeing her at the Dew Drop. And what did he

mean about tomorrow? Tomorrow was Saturday, and there was no school.

Beth caught her bus and sat in the back row, remembering her dream, and keeping an eye out the window, halfway expecting to see a hairy monster climb onto the back bumper. She laughed at herself, but still, the dream seemed to be almost real at times. There seemed to be some sort of beast pulling at her, bringing her down, and making her feel like an alien from outer space. And I thought this week was the turning point of my life on Cedar Island! she muttered to herself as she got off the bus and walked down the long driveway to her multisided house.

Shortly after they had moved in, she had counted the sides of the house. There were seventeen sides, or angles, depending on how you counted, and Mr. Kawaguchi had certainly fulfilled his ambition not to live in a box.

Mom knelt in the garden, clearing weeds from the flower beds. She looked up and said, "Hi, Beth. Put on the teakettle, would you? I'll be in after five more minutes."

"Sure," said Beth, tromping into the house.

There was a plate of brownies on the wooden counter, and Beth popped one in her mouth. They were thick and moist, and they reminded her of Rosie and the chocolate Milky Way bars she always ate for lunch. I'll take Rosie a brownie tonight, thought Beth, and put it into a sandwich bag while the water boiled.

"Tea!" she called through the back door.

"Be right in," said Mom, and Beth watched her slowly struggle to her feet. "Oh, my aching back," Mom said as she yanked off her garden gloves and stepped out of her big black boots. "I'm ready to relax. Thank goodness it's Friday."

Another boring weekend, thought Beth.

They sat at the table drinking tea. "How was your week?" asked Mom after pouring a second cup.

"Monday was the pits," said Beth. "Tuesday was great. I got to meet Alice Goddard, and Ted Sealley, and live through a storm."

"And go to the ASB meeting," Mom added.

And hear about the Fifties Dance, thought Beth, and probably not get an invitation to go.

"And Wednesday we all got to visit the Sealleys," Mom said. "I really enjoyed meeting them. I hope we get to know them better."

"Yeah," grunted Beth, thinking how much easier it would have been if she hadn't met Ted and Emily in front of the sign-up sheet for the writing contest. That was how her feelings for Ted had originally gotten all mixed up with hope.

"I've taken a brownie for Rosie," Beth said. "She and Jens are picking me up tonight to go to the Dew Drop."

"See!" Mom said with a smile. "I knew things would improve for you."

"Mom," wailed Beth. "You think it's an improvement going out with Rosie and her boyfriend? I'd rather stay home and read a book, than crash someone else's party."

"What's the party?"

"It's a benefit for the track team."

"Usually they want as many people as possible to come to a benefit," explained Mom. "It doesn't sound like you'll be crashing the party."

"I mean going with Rosie and Jens."

"Rosie wouldn't have invited you if she didn't want you to come."

There was no arguing with that statement. Rosie, as nice as she was, wasn't one to do something that she didn't want to do. And that was why Beth felt particularly good about the fact that she ate lunch with her everyday. It was good to think that someone like Rosie valued her friendship.

"Any ideas for the writing contest?" Mom asked.

Beth paused. "Nope. Not one. I've been too busy."

"You have been busy this week," Mom said. "I'm glad."

Beth peered into Mom's dark brown eyes. Mom had long eyelashes and cupid-shaped lips. In fact, Beth thought as she studied Mom's face, except for the wrinkles, and for the streaks of gray in Mom's hair, they really looked a whole lot alike. Except that Mom was always cheerful and smiling and Beth, well . . . Tell the truth to yourself, she muttered under her breath. If you can't tell the truth to yourself, who can you tell it to?

The truth was, Beth had become melancholy and shy since they moved, and knew that she looked on everything with a negative attitude. Although she hadn't always been this way, she couldn't seem to help herself. Only since December, since that fateful day when Dad sold the house in Bethesda and moved them to Cedar Island, Washington, had her personality changed. Often she thought that this new mood of hers was like the hairy monster of her dreams, trying to tear her apart.

"It's funny to think of writing," Beth said, "when I can't speak properly and I can never chit-chat with people."

"Don't worry about not speaking properly," Mom said. "You don't have to be a good speaker in order to write. Maybe the opposite is true. Lots of times people talk out their stories, and don't ever get around to writing them down."

Beth wondered whether to believe Mom, or to believe what Mrs. Atkinson said, that writing was as easy as speaking.

"I was going to suggest that you write your thoughts down as they come to you," continued Mom. "Maybe there's some way you could get an idea from them for a story."

"I'm still recording my dreams," Beth said.

"You could make up a story from one of your dreams," Mom suggested, nibbling another brownie despite the diet she was on. "Writing's easier if you write about what you know."

"Like what?" asked Beth.

"Like yourself. Write about yourself."

"Oh, Mom! Nobody wants to read about me. I'm nobody."

"Who's inside you saying that?" said Mom. Her voice shook as if she were trying not to yell. "That's not you talking. Not the real you at all. You are Beth Ann Hamilton, and you are a very important somebody."

Not somebody Ted Sealley would like, thought Beth grumpily. She picked up her books and started up the ladder to her loft.

"Think about it," Mom called when Beth reached the top. "Who is that person inside you saying all those nasty things?"

Is that my hairy monster? thought Beth. Could that be possible? Maybe he's angry because he doesn't like to hear me put him down. There, there, she said under her breath, feeling a giggle build up from the back of her throat. Maybe he's my own worst enemy besides being another part of myself. Okay, Mr. Monster, we'll be friends. It was strange, but somehow she felt better about herself after saying those words: We'll be friends!

Beth found Emily Summers's pencil on her desk. She reached for a piece of paper in her drawer and tried to write out her thoughts as she sat cross-legged on the bed. She used her Algebra book as a desk, but when she dotted her periods, she dotted so hard they poked right through into the cover of the book.

So there! Beth muttered under her breath. So there! She threw Emily's pencil onto her desk, then tore the paper into shreds and sprinkled it into the wastebasket.

Then Beth stood at her window and looked at the yard. The clouds had closed again and the world looked gray.

I wonder how track practice is going? she thought, watching a few drops of rain spatter on the ground. I wish I'd made track team. Then I'd see Ted every afternoon instead of only seeing him in Algebra.

Rosie's lucky she has Jens. They're so relaxed and comfortable with each other. I could ask Rosie if Ted and Emily are going together, but it's so obvious they have some connection with each other, it seems like a stupid question.

Oh, rats! thought Beth. Maybe I'm imagining everything, making up stories where none exist. Maybe Ted and Emily are only good friends.

Beth reached for her dream book. "My Own Worst Enemy," she wrote down. Not a bad title for a story, she thought, rereading her neat, tidy printing.

The rain began pounding onto the shake roof almost above her head. Rain! I hate it! thought Beth. I wish I'd stayed back East where I wouldn't have to look at that constant blur pelting past my window. She wiped her eyes. Was it only the rain blurring her vision? No, I won't cry, thought Beth. I'm not going to cry.

The telephone rang downstairs in the study.

"It's for you, dear," Mom called.

Beth wiped her eyes, hoping Mom wouldn't notice if they were a little red.

"Practice was shortened because of the rain," Rosie said on the other end of the line. "So I'm home and about ready to hop into the Jacuzzi. I just wanted to tell you we'll pick you up about quarter to eight."

"How was practice?" Beth asked, hoping Rosie would volunteer some information about Ted.

"My knees hurt," Rosie said. "When it started to pour, Coach sent us inside to work on the machines. I jerked my legs out on one of the machines and my knees locked. Nothing to worry about. At least it wasn't my ankles. A whirl in the Jacuzzi and I'll be good as new."

"Take care of yourself," Beth said. "You won't win any races if you hurt yourself."

"I know, I know, I know," Rosie said. "You're right, but I can't help it. I have a very bad habit of pushing myself beyond my limit."

"Next thing we know, you'll be taking pep pills or having your blood pumped up like some of the Olympic athletes," Beth said.

"No," Rosie said, but she started talking about a recent story involving a marathon runner who had a special diet that was supposed to build up his stamina so he could run thirty-six miles in the same time most people ran twenty-six.

Beth was listening with one ear when Mom came to the study door and jingled the car keys. "I'm going down to the ferry terminal to pick up Dad," she said.

Beth waved her hand good-bye.

"What are you wearing tonight?" Beth asked Rosie when Rosie paused for a breath.

"The same old thing, I suppose," Rosie said. "I hadn't thought about it, why?"

"Don't you have anything else to wear besides your sweats?" Beth asked.

"I do have a skirt I bought last year for my aunt's third wedding," Rosie said. "It's gray flannel and I could wear it with my gray sweater."

"Do you have nylons?"

"No way," Rosie said. "I can't stand them on my legs."

"Knee socks?"

"I could wear my gray knee socks," Rosie said, "but what's the point? I'd still be all in gray, just as if I wore sweats and my sweatshirt."

"Sorry to bug you," Beth said. "I just wondered if you ever got tired of wearing the same old thing all the time."

"One less thing to worry about," Rosie said cheerfully.

Beth laughed. "How right you are!"

They talked until Mom arrived home with Dad. Beth said quickly, "Hey, Rosie, I've gotta go. I'm not supposed to talk this long on the phone."

"Quarter to eight, don't forget," said Rosie, whose father was a psychiatrist and had given each of his six daughters their own telephone line so his would always be free for emergencies.

Beth put down the phone and ran out to kiss Dad on the cheek.

"How's my sweetheart?" Dad asked, leading the way into the kitchen.

"Fine," said Beth.

"Ready for *Washington Week in Review*, and *Wall Street Week*?" asked Dad, referring to their favorite programs on Channel Nine.

"I'm going out tonight," said Beth.

"How's that for our little girl?" Dad said, winking back at Mom who was already ladling stew into thick pottery bowls she had bought from an artist on the island.

"Where?" he asked, looking at Beth.

"The Dew Drop," said Beth. "It's no big deal, Dad." Except that Ted would certainly be there.

"Sounds like a super deal to me," said Dad. "It's your

first Friday night out on the town since we came west.''

Sure, thought Beth although she felt as if she were falling apart. I meet the boy of my life and he doesn't even tell me about the benefit, let alone ask me to go with him. Why? Because he's probably dating Emily Summers, who is gorgeous, number one, and talented, number two, and knows how to flirt, number three. Plain, ordinary me can't compete with someone like that. No way!

Beth took the bowl of stew and plunked down at the table. If I hadn't made a promise to Rosie, she thought, I'd be staying home and feeling sorry for myself. This way I get to go out and feel sorry for myself, but at least Mom and Dad don't have to feel sorry for me, too. They don't have to know how bad it really is!

Chapter Fourteen

Stupid me and my stupid promises, thought Beth, finding herself at eight o'clock in a wooden booth at the Dew Drop. Try as she might, Beth could not keep herself from leaning sideways so she could see whoever came in the front door.

"I wonder where Ted's at," Rosie said a little before nine o'clock. "And he helped set this benefit up. You'd think he'd come."

"Maybe he doesn't feel like a party," Jens said quietly. "So soon after his mom's death."

"He suggested the Fifties Dance," said Ray Nishimoto, who was also sitting at their booth. "I doubt if he'd have done that if he didn't want to go himself."

"He might have," Jens said. "It's a chance to make money for the ASB projects and give everyone some fun, too. Ted wouldn't let his own sadness interfere with that."

Beth sipped her Coke, and listened without saying a word as people talked and joked around her. Rosie introduced everyone who came past their booth, but the names buzzed in and out of Beth's head like nonsense words. She felt out of it, as if she would never be part of this group that had known each other since the days when their mothers pushed their buggies down the only sidewalk in the village. They laughed at "in" jokes that she couldn't possibly know the origin of, and said things that were a complete mystery to her.

When Rosie and Jens got up to dance to an old fifties song

blaring from the juke box, Phillip Predo slid into the seat next to Beth. She sipped on her Coke until the dregs gargled through her straw.

Phillip doodled on a napkin. He tipped back his beret and studied Beth with one eye.

"What are you doing?" Beth struggled with the words. Her stomach felt like a vacuum pump drawing in air until she had none left with which to speak.

Phillip handed her the napkin. It was a cartoon of Beth. Instead of words being surrounded by a bubble, to indicate her speaking, there was a bubble person in the Coke glass in which were the words: Let me out.

"Thanks," Beth said, not really knowing whether to feel pleased or not.

"Do you get it?" asked Phillip.

"Sure," she said.

"It's like a little gas bubble inside you trying to bounce out and be bright and cheery like everyone else, except the bigger it gets, the more you push it down, until it finally sucks you dry."

"Sure," Beth said in a sour tone, "I told you, I got it."

"No offense meant." Phillip tipped his beret forward.

"No offense taken," Beth said, wishing that Rosie and Jens would come back to the booth and talk to her so she wouldn't have to talk to this boob.

"Do you always go around looking like the world is eating you up?"

"Leave me alone," Beth said. "I'd like to see you come to a small school like Cedar Island High and get to know kids."

"What'd'ya mean?"

"I mean, I had to transfer here from my old school where I knew lots of people, and it just isn't that easy to make friends all over again."

"It sure isn't easy to make friends when you look down your nose at everyone," said Phillip. "You give everyone the impression that you're so superior. Like the ultimate judge of us all."

Beth suddenly remembered what Ted had said. Aloof. And there had been other remarks, too, in the past few days.

Remarks that indicated that people misunderstood her.

"I don't mean to give that impression," Beth said quietly, trying to keep from biting her lip. She felt totally rotten and wished she could dash out of the Dew Drop and sob in Jens's truck.

"You think you're shy, right?" Phillip doodled on a napkin, and avoided looking at her.

Beth nodded.

"You know what I think about your shyness?"

"I'm not a mind reader," Beth said sarcastically.

"I think your shyness is an attitude you've adopted so you don't have to feel left out, or so you don't have to put yourself out to talk to anyone."

"How do you know so much!" Beth's voice was quiet, but she seethed underneath, hating the implications of what Phillip was saying.

"I went to the School of Hard Knocks, too," said Phillip.

"You can't mean Cedar Island High," retorted Beth. "Or you don't know what you're talking about."

"I only got here in November."

Beth was astonished. Phillip seemed like someone who had lived here forever, like all the rest. She considered what he had said for a while as the music played on the juke box. Phillip drew curls on a napkin, like Emily's handwriting, although he added eyes and a curved mouth. Finally something clicked in Beth. What Phillip had said seemed right. I have pretended to be shy, she thought. I haven't been my regular, ordinary self because I've been so intimidated by everyone, thinking everyone else was clever, and I didn't want them to find out I wasn't as clever. I sure put out the wrong message. But how can I change it now?

"Do you know where Emily is?" Phillip picked up another napkin to doodle on.

"She's probably gone to the movies with Ted Sealley," Beth said, feeling bitter, but trying to keep a normal tone in her voice.

"Why would she do that?"

"Why not?"

"Going to the movies when there's a benefit for the track

team? I don't think Ted's the sort of person to do that. And I can't imagine Emily going to the movies with her cousin when there's a party on. She's such a party person.''

"Cousin?" Before she could stop herself, the word had jumped out of her mouth. Beth bit her bottom lip and tried not to blush.

"Didn't you know?" Phillip looked at her quizzically. "I thought everyone at Cedar Island High knew Ted and Emily were cousins."

"Cousins?" Beth repeated the word without thinking. "Cousins?"

"Uh-huh," Phillip said.

Then a flush of relief swept over Beth. Here I am, she thought, having an ordinary conversation, and I find out the answer to something that's been bugging me for days. Ted and Emily aren't going together, they're cousins!

Beth felt so happy she just had to dance, so she said to Phillip, "What are we doing, sitting here? Come on! Let's dance!"

She wished Ted were there to dance with, of course, but dancing with Phillip was better than sitting in the booth feeling sorry for herself.

After someone had changed the records in the juke box to more current ones, "Beat it" came on and Eggie appeared from nowhere.

"Dance?" he asked Beth, as she and Phillip were heading back to their booth.

She swung enthusiastically into Eggie's short arms. The top of Eggie's head came just to the tip of her nose, but he was a better dancer than Phillip, and Beth felt like dancing up a storm.

"Can I buy you a Coke?" Eggie asked when the music changed.

"Sure," Beth said. She sat down with him in a booth with Kit, a guy named Mark who looked like Gene Wilder, Lisa, and Gloria Davis, who wore a lead-gray dress covered with pockets, snaps, and zippers.

"Anyone seen Emily?" Phillip Predo poked his head into the booth.

"Her dad's coming home tonight after being away for two weeks," Kit said, refreshing Beth's memory of Emily's whereabouts. "She stayed home to see him."

That's right, Beth recalled, and then asked aloud, "Where's her dad been?"

"Saudi Arabia," answered Kit.

"Wouldn't I like to have a father like that," Lisa said as Phillip moved along to the next booth. "Mine thinks going to Seattle is a big deal."

"I hope you'll come to Math Club," Eggie was saying into Beth's left ear.

"I'm thinking about it," Beth said. "I'm not really keen on being in any math competitions, but I'd probably enjoy being in the club."

"We need a female representative," Eggie said. "Since we're such a small school, it's kind of hard to find a girl who's a hotshot in mathematics."

Beth wrinkled up her nose. "Does that mean you want a liberated woman to integrate the Math Club?"

"We don't want to be accused of being sexist," Eggie said.

"No way I'm going to join a club with a bunch of male chauvinists," Beth said firmly.

"I really want you to join Math Club," Eggie said slowly, his voice sounding a trifle hurt. "Your being female has no relevance, really. I didn't meant it that way."

"Oh!" Beth said with a sigh. "Don't mind me. I'm . . ." She was going to say, I'm just feeling sorry for myself because Ted's not here, and I've missed a perfect opportunity to take advantage of the fact that he's definitely not dating Emily.

"Feeling like a grouch?" finished Eggie, smiling broadly.

"Ooooh!" Beth said, pretending to frown.

Eggie sat up. "Let's dance again," he said, "and cut the dialogue. I'm no good with words anyway. Numbers is my line."

Beth laughed. She felt great in her new lilac-colored painter's pants and multi-colored purple, pink, and black cowl-neck sweater. She had pinned her hair back over one ear, and put on lipgloss. No eye makeup. She always thought her eyes were too big, and she didn't want them to look bigger with eyeliner.

"Oh, where is he," Rosie complained about three hours later. They were picking up their coats from the pile in the corner beside the juke box and getting ready to leave. "I don't believe it. The star of the track team can't even get his act together to show up for the benefit."

"Relax," Jens said, putting a heavily muscled arm across Rosie's back. Beth noticed the thickness of his fingers, and how the tips were grooved from hard work.

"I told Emily to remind him," Rosie said, "and she said she would. But you know her. Sometimes she can be a real airhead, herself."

"You know that Ted forgets his right foot from his left," said Jens, laughing. "You can't expect him to remember to come to a party, just because it's been planned for two weeks."

"I talked to him personally at practice today," Rosie said crossly.

"What did you say?" asked Beth, feeling as if her tongue was wobbling over the four simple words.

"I said: 'Remember the Friday Night benefit at the Dew Drop.' "

"That's clear enough," said Jens. "Maybe he had trouble with his car."

Maybe he was feeling sad about his mother, and couldn't face a crowd of happy people, thought Beth.

Brendon Bart lumbered in the door just as they were leaving. "Hi," he said to Beth. "What are you doing here?"

"Having fun," Beth said, and she meant it. "But what about you? You don't look in any shape for a party. You look exhausted."

"I've been helping Alice Goddard with the lambs," Brendon said with a huge yawn. "Snowflake, that big ewe of hers, had twins about an hour ago."

"You missed the party," said Rosie, punching a fist into Brendon's side. "You and Ted Sealley."

Brendon pulled a fiver out of the pocket of his thick,

brown lumber jacket, and tucked it into the rubber band around Rosie's ponytail. "Here's my contribution, anyway," he said.

"Oh, thanks Brendon," Rosie said, and chirping like a red-crested bird, she bounced out of the Dew Drop and into Jens's truck. Beth, Rosie, and Jens crowded together into the cab.

"I bet we made tons of money," Rosie chattered in the truck on the way home. "Did you see the crowd, Beth? Did you?"

Beth nodded and tried to share Rosie's enthusiasm, but she ached to see Ted and find out why he didn't show.

"I'm really glad you came," Rosie said and she patted Beth's knee.

"I am, too," Beth said, thinking, if I hadn't gone, I might never have found out that Emily and Ted were cousins. Cousins! Imagine!

"See you later," Jens said when he dropped her off at the Kawaguchi/Hamilton house.

"Thanks for taking me," Beth said.

"I'll call you tomorrow," Rosie said. "After I give Ted Sealley a huge hunk of my mind at track practice."

"Don't give him too much of your mind, sweetie," Jens said with a serious expression. He patted Rosie on the head. "Save some of it for yourself."

Rosie laughed and waved good-bye to Beth as Jens headed his truck down the driveway.

Beth studied the sky for a few minutes before going into the house. Stars twinkled. There were no clouds. Tomorrow is going to be an absolutely beautiful day, she thought with absolute certainty. I can feel it in my bones.

Chapter Fifteen

Cousins! reflected Beth as she lay in bed Saturday morning, watching the crystal blue sky through her loft window. To think that Emily and Ted were cousins all along, and I never even guessed. I'm really stupid. I could have asked Rosie and solved all my misgivings about Ted. What a dope I am! Well, just you wait until Monday morning, Ted Sealley, and I'll come on like you've never seen before. Aloof? Me? No way!

She picked up the dream notebook, which was under her pillow. The book opened automatically at the story she had titled, "My Own Worst Enemy."

Myself, wrote Beth.

Beth leaped off her bed, pulled on her thick down dressing gown and down booties, and sat at her desk. Emily Summer's United Airlines pencil sat in the jam jar Beth used as a pencil holder. It was bitten, chewed, and just right for writing a story.

Beth began, her hands flying over the paper. Page after page. She put aside her neat orderly printing and scribbled as fast as she could, letting the thoughts flow onto the paper, not worrying about what she was saying. Or how she was saying it. Or whether she was going to win. The important thing was just getting down the thoughts about how the big hairy monster was really the part of her that constantly put herself down, thought of herself as a failure, and was, indeed, her own worst enemy.

Her fingers cramped. She flexed them, stopping for a minute to focus her head. "You're not really stupid," she said suddenly, talking to the big hairy monster. "You're just like a little kid who grew up to be big and powerful without realizing what you were. You used all your energy in all the wrong ways, by putting yourself down for being stupid, instead of understanding that it's okay to be stupid sometimes!"

Beth dotted the last period.

"I'll leave it for a few days," she said, talking out loud to herself. "I'll do a better job of correcting my mistakes when I've been away from it for a while."

Beth climbed down her ladder into the kitchen and began making bran muffins, then she scrambled some eggs and made a pot of coffee. By the time breakfast was ready, Mom and Dad were up and dressed.

"You made breakfast! How wonderful!" said Mom, kissing Beth on the cheek.

"The start of a beautiful day," Dad said as he eagerly sipped his coffee. The rich aroma filled the room.

"It's spring," said Mom, sitting down at the table.

Beth looked through the octagon window at the Japanese garden. The vine maple was bursting with tiny red leaves. The white birches shimmered with yellow fuzz.

"Frank called last night while you were out," Mom said.

"It's all set for him to come out," Dad said.

Beth put down her muffin and clapped her hands. "Oh, goodie. When?"

"He'll be here the week before Easter, for your spring break, and stay through Sunday. He'll have to take the Red-Eye Flight at midnight after Easter."

Beth grinned. She was sorry to miss his call, but at least Frank would know that she wasn't spending every night alone at home feeling sorry for herself.

"I'm going for a walk," Beth said after she'd cleaned up

the kitchen and done her household chores. She put on her down jacket and heavy boots and went to the door.

"Have fun," Dad said.

"Don't get lost," Mom said.

Beth had always wanted to explore the wooded trail at the far end of their property line, but had never been fully motivated. She trudged through the dense, damp blackberry bushes, occasionally having to stomp on one in order to keep going. Stickers tugged at her jeans. Birds twittered in the evergreens. Yellow-orange fungus grew on moss-covered logs. And it smelled of vanilla and honey, ginger and cedar.

Beth broke through the woods onto a path leading alongside a bubbling creek. She was pretty sure she was heading in the right direction for Alice's house, and hoped she'd end up there.

Leaf mold lined the banks of the creek and cold water splashed over smooth stones. Beth pushed ahead, singing to herself. Less than an hour later, she burst through a hedge of huckleberry. Sure enough, there was Alice's sheep shed. Beth climbed on a bale of hay and saw two little balls of wool suckling the big old ewe.

"Hi!"

Beth nearly fell off the hay at the sound of the deep voice.

"Sorry," said the invisible voice. "Didn't mean to frighten you."

Brendon Bart popped up from the other side of the shed, his thick brown hair full of strands of hay. Hay also clung to his brown wool lumberman's jacket.

"Oh, hi," Beth said, and she giggled.

"What's wrong?" Brendon asked, spreading his hands up through his hair, scattering straw.

"Nothing," Beth said. "I was just surprised, that's all. I didn't expect to see anybody." She sure wasn't going to tell Brendon that his hay-covered jacket made him look like a teddy bear with the stuffing falling out.

"Where'd you come from?" Brendon asked, peering around to see if Beth had driven up in a car.

"There's a terrific trail down from my place," Beth said.

"I just started walking, and hoped I'd end up somewhere, and here I am." She raised her palms, spreading her arms wide.

"I can't believe it," Brendon said. "You, the new girl, follow a trail I've been wanting to follow for years."

"It's overgrown in lots of places," Beth said, realizing that she no longer minded when someone called her the new girl.

The two lambs finished nursing and starting jumping around the shelter of the lean-to.

Brendon climbed out. "I used to hike only so far on the trail," he said, "and then get stuck with the overgrowth. If you come down the trail before the blackberries have bushed out, it's probably not so bad."

"Why don't you walk home with me?" Beth asked, and then bit her bottom lip. What was she saying? What if Brendon thought she was coming on to him?

But Brendon said, "I'll have to wait to take the trail until I have some spare time, but then you'll find me at your back door. You live at Kawaguchi's, don't you?"

Beth nodded, no longer surprised at how many people knew where she lived. She reluctantly took her eyes off the two little balls of wools dancing and prancing around the pen. She couldn't believe that the lambs weren't even twenty-four hours old!

"It's beautiful here," Beth said, looking up into a burst of white blossoms on an old silver-barked cherry tree.

"Everything's started blooming since the storm," Brendon said, following her gaze.

"It really is lovely," Beth said, and she meant it. No more wishing for city streets and brick houses and her old school in Bethesda. She loved this little rock everyone called Cedar Island.

When one of the lambs squeaked, the mother ewe began snorting. Beth jumped back onto the hay bale to check if everything was all right. The lambs started nursing again, and Beth climbed down, and headed toward the verandah.

"Friend of yours in there," Brendon said as he pushed a

wheelbarrow of manure toward the vegetable garden.

Beth smiled. It was nice to think of Alice as a friend.

Beth went into the warm kitchen and was astonished to find Rosie sipping mint tea.

"Howdy," Rosie said. "I just tried to telephone you, but your line was busy. We must have mental telepathy."

Beth pulled up a chair and sat across from her red-headed friend.

"Did you see the newborn lambs?" Rosie asked.

"They're adorable," Beth said. "But what are you doing here? How come you're not at practice?"

"Practice was the pits," Rosie said. "I got Mom to drop me off here to get Gran to work on my ankles. They hurt like heck."

"Gran?" I don't believe it, thought Beth. Everybody has relatives all over the place.

"Alice is my mom's mom," Rosie said, "and Mom's taken her to the store for some groceries. She'll work on my aches and pains when she gets back."

"How does she do that?" Beth poured some tea into an empty mug sitting on the table.

"Sort of like massage," explained Rosie. "It's some old folk treatment she learned when she was in Alaska years ago. An old Eskimo lady taught her."

"I should come down here sometime and write down some of Alice's stories," Beth commented.

"She'd love it," Rosie said. "She's always been meaning to put down her adventures, but none of us is very interested in that sort of thing. You should mention it to her."

"I will," Beth said. "It'll give me something to do all summer."

"You might be occupied by Ted Sealley all summer," Rosie said mysteriously.

Beth felt as if she were turning the color of Rosie's hair.

"That man never gets any workout pains like I do," said Rosie, casually changing the subject. "But he sure has trouble with his head. You know what he said when I chewed him out at practice this morning?"

"What?" Beth asked.

"He said he got all mixed up because we had that day off with the storm, and he thought Friday was Thursday, and that's why he didn't get to the Dew Drop for the benefit."

"Oh!" Beth said, trying not to appear too interested.

"He was really annoyed when I told him," Rosie said.

"Everybody makes mistakes," Beth said.

"You know what he said?" Rosie wriggled her nose like a rabbit.

"What?"

"Guess."

"I hate guessing games," Beth said. "My mind fries and I can't think."

Rosie sipped her tea and looked at Beth over the rim of her cup. She put it down slowly on the scarred oak table, and said, "Ted said he was going to ask you to go with him."

"No!"

"Yes," Rosie said. "Cross my heart." She crossed both hands over her heart.

"Really?"

"Really and truly," Rosie said.

Beth put her cup onto the table. She pressed her hands together in her lap and squeezed so hard her knuckles cracked. "Really?" she asked again.

"I thought you had something going for Ted," Rosie said. "I wasn't sure, though, because you never said anything."

"You won't believe this," Beth confessed, "but I thought he might be going with Emily, and I didn't want to make a fool of myself over him if he was."

"He and Emily are cousins," Rosie said. "I can't believe I never told you."

"It never came up," Beth said.

"Well, listen," Rosie said. "I'll tell you something else, but you have to promise to act surprised."

"Go on." Beth sipped the last of her tea.

"Ted also said he was working up courage to ask you to the movie tonight, except he didn't really like what was playing at the Island Theater."

"I wouldn't care what the movie was," Beth said. "I'd see *Friday the Thirteenth* just to go out with Ted Sealley."

Rosie laughed. "I know the feeling, but I told Ted that Jens and I had rented a video of *Chariots of Fire* to show at home tonight, and that he could come and bring you. If he wanted to, that is."

"Rosie! You're setting me up!" Beth clanked her cup on the table.

"It's not as if he hadn't already said he wanted to ask you out."

Beth shook her head slowly. She felt all jumbled inside. It seemed strange that someone else knew Ted wanted to ask her out before she did, even if that someone was as neat a friend as Rosie. And what if it weren't true? What if Rosie was putting her on?

"You can always say no," Rosie said, "if Ted calls you, that is."

Beth felt a sudden urge to hurry home. What if Ted was already on the telephone, trying to get her?

"I was going to ask you anyway if you wanted to come over and see the movie," Rosie said.

"I'd love to," Beth said with a huge grin, "but let's wait and see what happens. I should go home now in case Ted is trying to call."

As Rosie walked with Beth to the door, they saw Mrs. McNeil, Rosie's plump, cheerful mother, walking up the path with Alice. Their arms were full of groceries.

"Hello, hello," Alice said. "Good-bye, good-bye. Do you have to leave so soon?"

"I'll come again," Beth said.

"Ted told me you were a writer," Alice said, wagging a gnarled finger at Beth. "Come and visit me, and bring your notebook. I'll fill it with stories."

Beth grinned and said, "I sure will." She hurried off the verandah, waving to Brendon, who was spreading fertilizer on the vegetable garden.

"See you Tuesday in Math Club," he called.

"Sure," Beth said. "I'll be there."

Beth took one last look at the lambs, then pushed her way onto the trail. The sun slanted through the trees. The birds sang. And Beth sang along with them.

Chapter Sixteen

"Ted Sealley called three times while you were gone," Dad said as soon as Beth came into the kitchen.

"Should I phone him back?" asked Beth, feeling breathless, and not necessarily from the hike home.

"It would be the polite thing to do. He was obviously anxious to reach you. I'm going out to see Mom in the garden," Dad said, taking his Windbreaker off the hook.

Beth hung up her coat, then went into the study and looked Ted's number up in the book.

"Hello?" His wonderful voice came over the wires.

"Hello," Beth said, her voice shaking. "This is Beth Hamilton."

"Hi," said Ted. "I feel like such a dope after last night, you can't imagine!"

"Yes, I can!" Beth said, feeling happiness well up inside her just at the sound of his voice.

"I bet you won't believe me when I tell you what happened, and why I missed the benefit for the track team."

"I'll believe you," Beth said, as if she didn't already know the reason.

"I got all mixed up on the days," Ted explained. "The storm got me all confused and I thought Friday was Thursday. Boy, do I feel stupid!"

"It's okay to be stupid," Beth said, thinking of her monster. "We all make mistakes."

"You must think I have cotton between my ears." Ted's voice sounded questioning, and Beth knew her opinion really mattered.

"Not at all," she said. "I do that number lots of times myself."

Ted laughed. Beth imagined his dimple deep in his right cheek. She imagined his green eyes shining. "To tell you the truth," he continued, "I'd be lost without Emily to keep me on track. Trouble was, last night her dad came home and she didn't go to the Dew Drop, so she forgot to remind me to go."

Beth felt like cheering. She didn't even feel jealous that Emily was so close to Ted that she helped him keep his act together. After all, they were cousins!

"It was really fun," Beth said, wishing, for the millionth time, that Ted *had* gone.

"Who'd you go with?"

"Rosie and Jens," she said, thinking that Ted had a funny catch in his voice. She waited, but he didn't say anything about having wanted to take her to the benefit.

"Are you going to join Math Club?" Ted asked.

"I just told Brendon today that I would," Beth said. "It might be fun, even though I hate competitions."

"Oh, yeah," Ted said. "You've been talking to Brendon?"

"Yes," Beth said. "I met him down at Alice's. I went down to see the new lambs. Did you know they were born last night?"

"Oh," said Ted. "You met Brendon when you went down to Alice's?"

"Yes," said Beth, thinking that, for some strange reason, Ted sounded relieved.

"How'd you get down to Alice's?" he asked.

"I followed a terrific trail through the woods and along a creek," Beth said. "It was almost like being in the wilderness."

"You'll have to show it to me."

"Be glad to," Beth said, and her heart thumped so hard she was sure Ted could hear it on the other end of the line.

"We've got lots of trails at this end of the island," Ted said. "Maybe you'd like to hike on them, too."

"I'd love to get to know this rock better," Beth agreed.

"I'm glad," Ted said simply, and by the tone of his voice, Beth felt like he really meant it.

There was a long pause. Beth searched her mind for something to say, but nothing came. It was almost as if all the little thoughts had bounced into a pan and fried together. She cleared her throat, but nothing came out.

"Would you like to go to a movie tonight?" Ted asked all of a sudden.

"Sure," Beth said, thinking, maybe what Rosie had said was true.

"We can go to the Island Theater," he continued, "or go to Rosie's and see *Chariots of Fire*. Whatever you want."

"I've seen *Chariots of Fire*," Beth said, "but I'd love to see it again."

"Me, too," Ted said. "I'm always up for a track movie."

Beth laughed and said, "I'll have to ask my folks. Can you hang on a minute?" Her palm stuck to the phone. She peeled it off and wiped her hand on her jeans as she hurried outside to find Mom or Dad.

"Sure," Mom said when Beth found her on her hands and knees weeding in a small flower garden.

"What time do I have to be home?"

"Whenever," Mom said. "I trust your judgment."

"Thanks," Beth said. "I won't be late."

Dad was burning the last bits of debris from the storm in the burn barrel. He waved at Beth as she hurried back into the house.

"Sorry to keep you waiting," she said breathlessly into the phone. "My folks were outside."

"That's okay," Ted said. "I'm just standing here chopping onions for Margot's Hot-Shot Chile . . ."

"And crying a little while he's at it," Margot called into the telephone.

"Hold a crust of bread in your mouth," Beth said. "It's

supposed to stop the onion juice from getting in your eyes.''

"Well," Ted said slowly, "can you go?"

"Yes." Beth grinned to herself. A date with Ted Sealley! I can't believe it. Me! Beth Ann Hamilton! She was so excited she almost shouted into the telephone. Luckily Ted distracted her by saying, "I'll pick you up at seven-thirty, if that's okay."

"Perfect," Beth said, although five-thirty would have been fine!

After she hung up, Beth took a long bath, using two of Mom's bath oil beads. Then she blow-dried her hair, and snipped a little more off her bangs so they didn't cover her eyebrows. She pinned one side back as she had for the benefit, and experimented with Mom's eye makeup. It makes me look like an orphan, she thought, amazed at how huge her dark eyes seemed with a little liner around them. Oh, well! I'll try it once.

Mom and Dad had come in from the garden and were both in the kitchen preparing dinner. Mom's cheeks were rosy and Dad looked relaxed and happy.

My lucky day, Beth thought, feeling a warm glow as she climbed her ladder to get dressed for her first date. I made friends with my big hairy monster, and now I'm about to make friends with Ted Sealley.

Beth didn't know what to wear. Finally she decided on the red cotton cords Mom had given her for Christmas, and which she hadn't worn to school yet, and a nubby gray-and-red-striped cotton pullover.

"Look at our daughter, Nora," Dad said when Beth climbed down her ladder into the kitchen. "Isn't she beautiful!"

Mom turned around from the stove. "My," she exclaimed, and her dark eyes glistened. "You look very special, my dear."

"Thank you, thank you," Beth said, nodding to first Mom and then Dad, as if she were royalty. "And I feel very special, too."

"Where are you going?" Dad asked when they sat down to dinner.

"To Rosie's, to watch a video."

Mom and Dad exchanged glances across the table.

"Hmm," Dad said, clearing his throat. "Will someone be home?"

"Oh, Dad," Beth said. "You know Rosie has five sisters. There's bound to be someone home."

"I don't feel very good about your going to someone's house unless I'm sure there will be adults around," Mom said.

"You mean I can't go?" wailed Beth, dropping her fork to her plate. "I can't call Ted after I already said yes, and tell him my folks won't let me go. You never asked me where I was going and I didn't think it mattered. I mean, I'm not about to do anything crazy."

"I think Beth's old enough to know right from wrong," Dad said, looking at Mom.

"I do, too," Mom said, nodding slowly, looking into Dad's eyes.

Beth usually felt shut out and isolated when her parents looked at each other like that, but today she smiled and thought that in half an hour, she was going to be out with none other than Ted Sealley!

Chapter Seventeen

Beth answered the door. Ted wore brown cords and a cream-colored, hand-knit sweater. He had on a green Windbreaker with TRACK written in block white letters across the back. His white-blond hair was parted on the left-hand side, and Beth realized with a shock that it was the first time she had seen his hair parted and combed. Usually it tumbled all over his head, and past his ears.

"Hi," she said, opening the door wide.

Ted handed her a small purple crocus and said, "The first of the season."

"Thank you." Beth looked at him and their eyes met. No more words seemed necessary.

"Come and say hi to my folks," she said. While Ted was talking with them, she went into the bathroom and pinned the crocus in her hair.

Ted grinned when she returned. Beth nodded to Mom and Dad and said, "We won't be late."

"I can't be late anyway," Ted said. "I've got work to do tomorrow."

"On Sunday?" asked Mom.

"I work for my dad," Ted said. "I wind mandrels for him for this new probe he's designed. You won't believe it, but he uses big, fat plastic hair curlers and winds silastic tubing on them."

"I don't understand a word you're saying," Mom said, grinning, "but it sounds impressive."

"It's like this," Ted said, holding his hands in a cylindrical shape. "The probe is something he designed to measure dissolved gas."

Beth watched Mom's eyes glaze over. She felt the same way, but didn't want to interrupt Ted.

"I'd love to see your dad's set-up sometime," Dad said. "It sounds fascinating."

"He's pretty busy," Ted said, "but I know you'd be welcome to stop by."

Beth got her down jacket, and Ted followed her to the door. Mom and Dad both walked to the back porch behind them. It made Beth feel funny, as if they didn't trust Ted, or something.

"It's been really nice seeing you both again," Ted said, shaking Dad's hand.

"And you, too," Mom said.

Ted opened the door of his Plymouth for Beth, who slipped in, wishing she had the nerve to slide all the way over to his side.

"Hi, over there," Ted said with a grin as he climbed into his side. He tilted his head to the left. "How'd you like to move closer? This side is a little warmer than that one."

Beth looked up to the porch. Mom and Dad had gone back inside. She didn't want them to think she was being pushy on the first date, but Ted's words were too difficult to resist. She moved until she was almost close enough to touch him.

"That's better," Ted said softly, grinning down at her. "Now it feels like a real date."

Beth couldn't help herself. She laughed out loud.

"What's the joke?" asked Ted as he started the old engine.

"I couldn't tell you what a real date feels like," Beth said, then bit her tongue. Rats! she thought. The last thing I need to do is let Ted know I've been a failure with boys.

"Didn't you go out when you lived back East?"

Beth shook her head. "Not really. I hung around with a group of kids and we always did things together. We'd been friends all through our freshman and sophomore years, so it wasn't exactly what you could call dating.''

"Just goes to show," Ted said, shaking his head slowly, turning onto the main road from the driveway. "Here I thought you must be a very sophisticated lady, with tons of experience."

"Me?" Beth said incredulously.

"You," Ted said.

"I sure must have given a lot of people the wrong impression about me," Beth confessed. "I'm not the least bit sophisticated. I never had a date before, unless you count the time I went with a boy to the Smithsonian Institute, and I only went with him because no one else in the crowd wanted to go, and he didn't want to go alone."

"Is it sort of dangerous to go out alone back East?" asked Ted.

"I never thought so," Beth said. "Some people say it is, but I never had any trouble."

"Course it's not New York or Washington, D.C.," Ted said.

"Bethesda, where I'm from, is on the outskirts of Washington, D.C.," explained Beth. "The Smithsonian is right in the center of Washington."

"You see," Ted said as he wheeled the car down the black-topped road, "I've learned something already and that must mean that you are more sophisticated than I am."

Beth patted his arm as Ted pulled into the McNeils' driveway. He stopped the car and took his key out of the ignition.

"Don't go comparing yourself to me," Beth said softly. "I may be more sophisticated in some things, but you know more about winding mandrels."

Ted laughed. "I bet you don't even know what a mandrel is."

"I don't," Beth said.

"Well I'm going to show you. You come over with your mom and dad tomorrow, and I'll give you a little demonstration."

"Mom's singing in church," Beth said, feeling the disappointment mount in her.

"Come in the afternoon."

"I think she's practicing with Mr. Bellga's band," she said, crossing her fingers, hoping it'd give Ted the hint to ask her to the dance.

"Oh, yeah?" Ted looked interested, and Beth was about to elaborate, but Jens appeared at the double-width front door.

"Come on, you two." Jens sounded as if he were trying to make himself heard above crashing waves. "You're holding up the works."

"Come in," Rosie said when they entered. "We were wondering when you'd stop necking in the car and come to watch the movie."

"Oh, Rosie!" blurted Beth. "We weren't!" Beth was sure she was the same color as the purple crocus in her hair.

Jens put his large hand across Rosie's face. "Don't mind her," he said. "She's just so happy you're both here together, that she doesn't know what she's saying."

"Uh-huh," Rosie said, flipping her ponytail up and down. "Jens is right. And now that you are here, let's get some popcorn and go to the movies."

The McNeil house was huge. Each of the six girls had a bedroom and bathroom of her own. Their parents' room was in a separate wing. The large kitchen was in the center of the house, just slightly to the left of the front door. All across the front of the house windows looked onto the beach, which was lit by floodlamps. A fourteen-foot sailing dinghy bobbed at the side of a floating pier. The house was all wood and stone, with beautiful Oriental scrolls hanging on the walls, and Persian rugs lining the floors.

"Come on," Rosie said as she picked up a ceramic bowl full of popcorn. "Let's go into the family room."

She led the way down a long hall with bedrooms off both sides. At the very end was another large room lined with bookshelves, and filled with soft cushions, a basket swinging chair, and a long overstuffed couch. As in the other rooms, a window covered the side of the house facing the beach. The water lapped onto the shallow rocky shore and Beth almost wished they could just sit and watch the sea, rather than turning on the video.

A large video screen stood in front of the window. Rosie pulled the drapes, and Ted and Jens lifted the couch so it faced the screen, rather than the huge stone fireplace along the end wall.

Ted dropped into the corner of the couch. He smiled up at Beth and patted the spot next to him.

"Are we ready?" Jens asked. He stood by the door with his hand on the light switch.

"Just a sec," Rosie said. "I was supposed to tell Susie and Lillie." Rosie left the room while Beth walked toward the couch.

"I won't bite," Ted said, patting the seat again.

Beth felt nervous. Her feelings for Ted, so long submerged because she thought he was totally out of her class, and also going with Emily, had suddenly surfaced with his attention, and she wasn't sure she trusted herself. What she really wanted to do was sit on his lap and forget the movie.

Ted stood up and reached for Beth's hand, pulling her toward the couch. He turned around and, with his hands on her shoulders, he gently pushed her down. Her rear end hit the soft sunken cushion. She grinned.

"See," he said. "I don't bite."

"I know," she said. "It's just that I feel overwhelmed." There. The truth was out.

He patted her knee. "Did I tell you yet how nice you looked tonight?"

Beth shook her head.

"Did I tell you that I've been wanting to ask you out since I first saw you at school?"

"No," Beth said. And then she asked in a wondering voice, "Why?"

"It gets sort of boring hanging out with the same old people all the time," said Ted. "And you looked like a person I would really want to know."

His hand was still on her knee. Beth slipped her hand into his and said, "You're someone I've really wanted to know, too."

At that moment, Rosie returned with two of her sisters. "This is Susie," she said, introducing a red-haired girl about her size, with freckles across her upturned nose, "and Lillie," Rosie said, pointing to the other red-haired girl, about twenty years old.

"Hi," said Beth and Ted in unison, and then they looked at each other and slapped hands—first the right, then the left, then both together.

"Boy," said Rosie, shaking her ponytail. "You sure are two of a kind."

Beth looked at Ted and grinned.

After Jens had turned off the lights and Rosie had switched on the video, *Chariots of Fire* came on the screen, and the music filled the large comfortable room. As Susie and Lillie snuggled into the overstuffed couch, along with Rosie and Jens, Beth and Ted were forced to move closer together. Ted lifted his right arm and Beth snuggled up against him. He tucked his arm around her shoulders and she felt truly wonderful.

"Where's the popcorn?" asked Rosie about one-third of the way through.

Susie pushed herself out of the couch and went over to one of the bookcases. "Now it's cold," she said.

"We could turn it off and make more," Jens suggested.

"I like cold popcorn," Rosie said.

"And Milky Way bars," Beth added.

"It's amazing, isn't it," Lillie said, "that Rosie can eat so much junk, and still not put on weight?"

Everyone laughed at Lillie's tone of voice, and because she was obviously struggling to keep her own weight down.

"Popcorn anyone?" Rosie passed the bowl.

"Ted looks a little like Eric Liddell, don't you think?" Rosie said as the Scottish runner picked himself up after being pushed down on the track. "And has the same sort of drive."

"Maybe Ted was Eric in another lifetime," Lillie said.

"Whoa!" Ted said. "Don't lay that on me!"

Beth couldn't take her eyes off the screen. Even with Ted's arm over her shoulders, creating a warm cosy feeling, the movie touched her, and she felt as if she were really living in those days after the First World War.

After the movie, Jens turned on the lights, Susie and Lillie left the room, and Rosie asked, "Ice cream, anyone?"

"Me!" Ted said.

"Me, too," Beth said.

"Jens bought a carton," said Rosie. "It's in the kitchen."

They returned to the center of the house.

"Not licorice, I hope," Ted said when Rosie took a gallon carton out of the freezer.

Ted, Jens, and Rosie laughed. Before Beth could say, "What's the joke," Jens turned to her and said, "They think I'm the only one on Cedar Island who likes licorice. They've teased me about it for years. Do you like licorice, by any chance?"

Jens looked so little-boyish that Beth felt like teasing him by saying no. But she told the truth. "I love licorice," she said. "I like it better than chocolate."

"Better than chocolate?" Rosie and Ted said in unison.

"I knew it," said Jens. "I knew she was my kind of person."

"Now, now," said Rosie. "Don't go overboard." And she smiled at Beth as if to say: Only teasing. You know I'm not jealous of you.

Words are so impossible sometimes, thought Beth, as Rosie dished out four big bowls of hand-cranked chocolate ice cream. They can convey the wrong meaning if not used carefully. I can't wait to go over my big hairy monster story, and be sure I've said it just right. I want to write exactly what I mean.

"Are you daydreaming?" Ted whispered in her ear.

Beth looked up. His dimple deepened and she couldn't resist. She raised her finger to press it into the indentation. The tip of her finger disappeared.

They ate, joked, talked, and ate again until there wasn't a lick of ice cream left.

"If we don't leave soon," Beth said, after checking the clock above the stove, "I'm going to have a curfew."

"I turn into a pumpkin at midnight, anyway," Ted said, and he returned down the hall to the family room to get their coats.

"Having fun?" asked Rosie in a soft voice when Ted left the kitchen.

Beth nodded.

"I'm really glad you and Ted came over tonight. If you want, we'll try to get another video for next Saturday night."

"I don't want to rush anything," Beth said, keeping her voice quiet although Ted was at the far end of the house.

"It doesn't look to me like you would be," Rosie said. She raised her eyes to Jens and said, "What do you think, sweetie?"

Jens put his big hand across Rosie's mouth. "I think you need to butt out," he said. "In other words, mind your own business."

Rosie bounced her ponytail from side to side. She wrinkled up her nose at Beth, and Beth wrinkled her nose back. Then they both started laughing, and when Ted returned, they had broken into full-scale giggles.

"Don't mind them," Jens said, looking at Ted. "They're nuts."

Beth let Ted put on her coat, and just before she followed him out the door to the car, she turned and hugged Rosie. "If we're nuts," Beth said, "it feels great."

"Stay with the feeling," Rosie whispered, hugging Beth back. "It can only get better!"

Chapter Eighteen

On Sunday morning, Beth sat in church with Dad as Mom sang in the choir. Afterwards Mom was going to practice with Mr. Bellga and the band.

Mom's singing at the school dance, thought Beth, and I don't even get to go. Unless Ted asks me. If he remembers to ask anyone.

"Do you want to go over to the Sealleys', Dad?" Beth asked when they were driving home from church. "You remember Ted said it would be okay."

"I'd love to," Dad said, "if you don't think we'd be imposing."

"We don't have to stay long," Beth said, although when they got there, and Ted showed them through his father's workshop, she wished they could stay all day.

Across the Sound, the Cascade Mountain Range was like a backdrop behind Seattle. Southeast, Mount Rainier seemed to hang from the sky.

"Another beautiful day," Ted said. "And would I love to be out sailing!"

"Me, too," Beth said. "Rosie promised to take me out in their dinghy some day."

A large ketch slipped by in front of the house. Someone waved from the bow. Ted stood on the edge of the cliff,

111

waving back. "That's Emily," he said. "She's out in her dad's boat."

"She's so lucky," Beth said with a sigh. "I'd love to be able to go out in a big sailboat like that."

"I'm sure she'd be glad to take you," Ted said. "Now that her dad's home, they'll probably go out every weekend."

"Do they take long trips with their boat?" Beth asked, trying to hide the longing in her voice.

"Every summer," Ted said. "Margot and I used to go with them all the time. But now I work for Dad when I'm not in training, and Margot's taking summer courses."

"I'd like to take a writing course this summer," Beth said. "Do you know of any around?"

"I know the winner of the writing contest gets to go to one at the University," Ted said.

"Won't be me." Beth felt the sides of her mouth slide down.

"Don't put yourself down," Ted said.

"I'm just being truthful," Beth said wistfully.

"Try being positive instead."

She turned so that her back was to the view.

Stepping sideways until he faced her, Ted put his hands on her shoulders and shook them slightly. "So what's so important about winning?" he asked.

Beth shrugged.

"Think about it," Ted insisted.

"If you don't win your track meet, then you don't get to go to the state meets, do you?"

"So what?"

"Yeah, but isn't that fun? I mean, don't you really like to go?"

"Yes, I really like to go," Ted said. "But it's not a matter of life and death for me. If I'm good enough, I get to go. Otherwise I'll stay home and do something else."

"Like wind silastic tubing on hair curlers for your dad?"

Ted laughed. "You're getting it," he said, and reached out to pat her head.

Beth ducked. In the abruptness of her motion, she lost her

footing. Quick as a wink, Ted caught her in his arms as she fell forward.

"Careful," he said, whispering into her hair. "You might have gone over the cliff."

Feeling the salt wind off the beach ruffle her hair, Beth looked up at Ted's white-blond hair, which seemed bleached in the spring sunshine.

"What's so important about winning?" he asked again.

Beth bit her bottom lip. "I guess winning isn't so important," she said. "It's knowing that you've done your best."

"Now you sound like Mr. George, the principal," Ted said, and he took her hand and started walking back to the house.

"I can't figure out why everybody around here has such a positive attitude about everything," Beth said as they returned to the workshop.

"It's partly because of Mr. George," Ted said. "He figures that we should all get off the rock someday, and make our way in the world. He wants us to have all the confidence we need."

"You sure seem to," Beth said, wishing she could have half of what Ted had.

"He's drilled into all of us, over and over, that if we win, it doesn't necessarily mean that we're a success. And if we lose, it doesn't necessarily mean that we're a failure."

"I'm beginning to understand," Beth said slowly, thinking about her story for the contest, and how she'd revise it a little to include some of the things Ted was saying.

"Success," Ted added, "depends on where you were when you started, and how far you've come."

"Well, I've come from Bethesda, Maryland," said Beth, joking, "and I'm feeling pretty good right now. I guess I'd define success as feeling good about yourself."

"Right on," Ted said. "Right on!" And he bent over and kissed Beth on the forehead.

Someday, she thought, he's going to kiss me on the lips, and I'm going to faint.

"See you at school tomorrow," said Ted as both fathers came out of Mr. Sealley's workshop.

"See you," said Beth, and for once, she could hardly wait until Monday.

Chapter Nineteen

Before classes on Monday morning, Beth looked for Ted in the halls, but to no avail. She looked for him in the cafeteria during lunch, until Rosie finally interrupted her thoughts and said, "He works out in the gym at noon every day."

"Who?" Beth asked, pretending ignorance.

"Who else?" said Rosie, tossing her ponytail around her head.

"Hmm," Beth said, creasing her forehead, pretending to think. "You wouldn't be referring to Ted Sealley by any chance, would you?"

Rosie giggled and said, "None other."

Before they could continue the conversation, Emily Summers came up to their table. She wore a mauve leotard top, a black cardigan, and baggy black pants that billowed around her legs, and tightened again at the ankles.

"Hi," Beth said, feeling more friendly toward Emily than she ever had before. "Want to join us?"

"I was wondering if you had the ASB minutes," said Emily. "We're having a meeting with Mr. George to discuss the May Day Dance, and I should be there with the book."

"It's in my locker," Beth said.

Emily pulled out a chair, turned it around, and sat on it backward, her long legs straddling the chair. She pushed a hand up through her frizzy blond hair, and said in her dramatic voice, "No prob. I can get it after you finish lunch."

115

"Aren't you eating?" Rosie asked as she munched on her Milky Way.

"I forgot my lunch," Emily said. "But who are you to talk about eating?"

"Don't you start in on me, too," Rosie said. "Candy bars are my passion and I don't see what's wrong with having one for lunch. It sure saves time making sandwiches."

"Here," Beth said, handing Emily half of her favorite sandwich, cheese with mayonnaise and lettuce on wheat berry bread.

"You're a doll," Emily said, and she munched on the half sandwich as if she hadn't eaten for forty-eight hours.

When they finished, Rosie went over to talk to Kit and Lisa, and Beth said to Emily, "Let's get that notebook."

As they were leaving the cafeteria, Beth said, "I saw you on your sailboat yesterday. Did you have fun?"

"We had a blast," Emily said. "Would you like to come sailing with us one day during Easter Break?"

Beth nodded and grinned. Emily must have been reading her mind.

"You wouldn't be afraid?"

"Gosh no," Beth said. "Why would I?"

"Sometimes people are. I mean, I thought people who lived back East never got on the water much, and might, you know . . ." Emily clicked her tongue against the roof of her mouth in disgust. "Oh, forget it!" she said. "I never say the right thing at the right time."

"Don't worry about it," said Beth in a soothing voice. "I'm always putting my foot in my mouth."

Emily lifted her foot out of her clog and twirled it in the air. She was, of course, wearing mauve-and-black-striped socks, and Beth wished, for the merest fraction of a second, that she could be as glamorous and dramatic as Emily Summers.

"Can you get it in your mouth?" Beth asked, laughing.

Emily grabbed her ankle and, in the struggle to get her foot up to her mouth, fell on the floor.

Beth immediately bent over to help her up. "Are you okay? I didn't mean to set you up for that!"

"My own stupid fault," Emily said, struggling to her feet

and rubbing her rear end. "I'm always getting into trouble because I'm trying to impress somebody."

"You don't have to impress me," Beth said, astonished. Why would someone like Emily Summers want to impress her?

"I wanted to," Emily said.

"Why?" I can't believe I'm hearing this, thought Beth.

"Because you seem so self-contained, so confident and mature," Emily said.

Beth shook her head in amazement. "If you only knew . . ." she began.

"I mean, I'm always leaving stuff everywhere, and I always seem to be so disorganized and you, well . . ." Emily paused and flipped her hands through her frizzy blond hair. "You seem to be so content with yourself the way you are. And even though you didn't know anybody here at school, it didn't seem to bother you a bit."

You're 100 percent wrong, Beth wanted to shout. How could anyone possibly think that?

"I hope I haven't offended you by saying all this," Emily said. "But that's how you seem to me, and that's why I wanted to impress you."

"I don't mind you saying it," Beth said slowly, trying to find the right words. "But that's not how it's been for me at all. I've been feeling totally out of it ever since I moved to Cedar Island. I guess I've given some people the impression that I'm aloof, but that's not true."

Beth and Emily walked a little farther down the hall, and suddenly Beth said with a burst of emotion, "The truth is, I've been scared most of the time and didn't know how to meet people. If it hadn't been for Rosie, I'd have died of loneliness."

Emily said nothing, but she hooked her arm in Beth's as they headed down the hall to Beth's locker.

"I really meant that about taking you sailing," Emily said sincerely as Beth handed over the ASB notebook.

"I'd love to come," Beth said happily, feeling as if she had made another friend.

Emily closed one large green eye. "I'd ask Ted, too," she

said. "But he, Margot, and Uncle Sam are going to Hawaii for Easter Break."

Beth tried to control the corners of her mouth, but they slipped down. All her good feelings about having Emily invite her sailing disappeared in the knowledge that Ted was going away.

"That's okay," Emily said. "They'll only be gone a week."

"It's nice that they can get away," Beth said, trying to show some enthusiasm.

"You bet! Christmas was a real bummer, and they need to get away and have some fun." Emily banged her clogs on the floor as if to emphasize her statement.

The bell rang. "See you later," Beth called, and hurried off to class, wishing it were Algebra, counting the minutes until last period.

When it was finally time for Algebra, Beth was so intent on looking for Ted in the back row, that she didn't notice until she sat down that Ted was sitting in the seat next to her.

"Hi," Ted said warmly. "How are you?"

"Fine." Beth opened her notebook with trembling hands.

"I wish I could drive you home after school," Ted said, "but we've got track practice in preparation for the big meet this coming Saturday."

"It's the thought that counts," Beth said, smiling.

"Will you come to the meet?"

"I'd love to," Beth said, not wanting to tell him that she wouldn't miss it for the world.

"It might be boring for you," Ted said.

"Don't worry about it," Beth said teasingly. "If it's boring, I'll leave."

"Don't leave without telling me where you're going," Ted said. "Promise?"

"I promise," Beth said, thinking that this promise would be an easy one to keep.

On Tuesday after school Beth kept her promise and went to Math Club with Brendon, Eggie, and five other male students. It didn't bother her in the least that she was the only girl.

Mr. Ives explained conversions from Fahrenheit to centigrade and back again, and then gave them several problems. This isn't that hard, Beth thought as she breezed through the work.

Then Mr. Ives asked them to figure out how to set up a linear conversion scale using logarithms. Beth got out her calculator and her log book, and tried to remember various things Frank had shown her, but to no avail. Eggie was grinning to himself and obviously having a blast. Brendon and the other students frowned as they bent over their papers.

Finally Mr. Ives showed them how to set up the scale. Eggie hooted with delight when he realized that he was the only one who had come near to solving the problem.

"Don't worry about it," Mr. Ives said to the others. "I was just getting you used to a process of thinking. I doubt if there will be anything quite that hard in the competition."

Beth picked up her books and moved to the door.

"Thank you for coming, Miss Hamilton," Mr. Ives said. "I hope we haven't, as the saying goes, turned you off."

"It was fun," Beth admitted.

"Will we have the pleasure of your company again?"

"I'll try to come," said Beth, "but I can't promise." Promising would mean she'd have to commit herself to doing it, and Beth still wasn't sure she wanted to get involved in Math Club. There seemed so many new possibilities opening up for her all of a sudden, that she wanted to be free to try anything else new that might come along.

Beth walked over to the stadium. Ted was talking to Coach, and as soon as he saw Beth, he picked up his tote bag and hurried over.

"Am I ever glad to see you," he said, and his dimple deepened.

"I'm glad to see you, too," Beth said, conscious of the fact that she looked stylish in her jeans and coral-red sweatshirt.

"Can I take you home?" asked Ted.

Beth nodded.

"Race you to the car," Ted said, then took off at a clip.

Beth followed, loving the feel of the wind lifting her hair, her legs striding forward, her heart pumping from the exertion. By the time she reached the Plymouth, her eyes were watering.

Ted sat crosslegged on the roof of the car, clapping and cheering.

Beth closed her fists, and raised them in a victory salute.

Chapter Twenty

Just as Beth was setting the table for dinner Friday night, the phone rang in the study. She dropped the silverware and ran to answer it.

"Hi," Ted said. "Hope I haven't interrupted anything."

"No," Beth said, her heart heating wildly. "How are you?"

"Looking forward to the big meet tomorrow," Ted said. "I was just, well, I mean, I was hoping that you'd be there."

"I wouldn't miss it," Beth said truthfully. She wanted to add: "I can't wait to see you run," but Ted continued to speak.

"I wanted to give you a ride over there," he said, "but I've got to get to the stadium early."

"That's okay," Beth said. "I'll get there somehow."

"Maybe Jens could pick you up in his truck."

"I don't think he's going to the meet," Beth replied. "Rosie said he's working overtime. They're trying to get the boat ready to take off for Alaska the day after Easter."

"That's reminds me to tell you," Ted said. "Dad, Margot and I are going to Hawaii for Easter."

"Emily told me," said Beth, relieved that Ted thought to tell her himself.

"That cousin of mine! She never leaves any surprises," Ted said in a mock-grumpy voice.

"I'm glad you get to go," Beth said quickly, hoping to distract him from any bad feelings toward Emily.

"Me too," said Ted, and then there was a long pause. Beth desperately wanted to say something, anything, to say how she understood about their wanting to get away for the holidays, but any words seemed superficial. And to tell the truth, part of her wished he wasn't going and that he'd be home to spend time with her. And to meet Frank.

"Emily said she plans to take you sailing," Ted said, breaking the silence.

"Oh! I hope she does!" Beth blurted, and then bit her bottom lip, hoping she hadn't come on too strong.

There was another long silence. Beth scoured her brain, trying to find things to say, and then she realized with a start, that maybe Ted was stammering because he felt uneasy talking to her. How weird! she thought. As if I were anybody important.

As if I were anybody important! she repeated, catching herself. That's a put-down, she muttered under her breath, and I'm not into put-downs anymore.

"This conversation is getting nowhere," Ted said finally. "I hope you don't think I'm a nerd, or anything, but I hate the telephone. It seems too darned impersonal. If I were standing in front of you I wouldn't have any trouble thinking of things to say, but this machine gives me the creeps."

Beth giggled, and the ice was broken.

They talked and talked, and laughed, and then Ted said, "Margot's going to be on my case if I don't get dinner started. It's my turn to cook tonight, but—oh! what I meant to ask you was, can you go out for dinner with me tomorrow night? I thought we could go to a little Mexican restaurant I know of in the city."

"I'd love to," Beth said breathlessly.

"If it's okay with you," said Ted, "we'll leave right after the track meet."

Of course it's okay! thought Beth, and said out loud, "I'll be ready!"

After they had said good-bye, Beth put down the phone

and twirled around the study, feeling totally ecstatic. She was going to dinner in Seattle with Ted!

When Beth asked Mom and Dad's permission, Dad said, "He seems like a nice young man. I can't think of any reason for you not to go."

Beth agreed with that statement 100 percent.

Saturday morning was bright and clear. There were a few small clouds drifting in the northern part of the sky, but the Olympic Mountains to the west were visible and sparkling with the last of the winter snow.

Emily called just as Beth was mixing up bran muffins for breakfast.

"Could you write up the track meet for the paper?" Emily asked.

"Sure," Beth replied. "I'd be glad to. But aren't you going?"

"My dad wants to take Mom and me shopping in Seattle," Emily said. "He's itching to spend some money on his girls, he says."

"That's great," Beth said.

"You bet," Emily said. "I could do with a new outfit. I'm sick of wearing all the same old stuff."

"Your clothes look great on you," Beth said, wishing she looked as good in her "old stuff" as Emily did.

"Hey," Emily said, "it's nice of you to say so. I don't agree with you, but thanks anyway."

When they hung up, Beth thought, What's with Emily? She sounds like a worse case than I was. I don't think anybody can put her down more than she already puts herself down. I wonder why? She's got everything going for her. Looks, brains, money, personality. Just goes to show, I guess, it's not what you've got going for you that counts, but how you think about it.

Beth got the muffins out of the oven just as Mom and Dad came into the kitchen. She poured them each a big mug of coffee, and then scrambled some eggs.

Beth could hardly wait until twelve-thirty, when Dad was

to drive her up to the school. It seemed years instead of only a week since she and Ted had gone to Rosie's together to see *Chariots of Fire*. And it seemed centuries since the day she had tried out for the track team and made such a miserable fool of herself.

At least I tried, Beth consoled herself as she got a notebook and pen ready to record all the information she needed for an article for the paper.

At the stadium, Beth looked all over for Ted, but couldn't find him. She stood by Rosie who wore a bright scarlet headband that clashed with her hair.

"The first race is mine," Rosie said as she screwed the last spike into her track shoes.

"What is it?" Beth asked, holding her pencil to her notebook.

"It's the two mile, or three thousand two hundred meter," said Rosie. "Look!" She drew up the sleeve of her green sweatshirt, showing Beth her right arm covered with numbers written in black felt pen. "My times from last year. I'm out to beat my own record."

"Why so many numbers?" Beth asked.

"One for each lap and there's eight laps. This way I know if I have to speed up at the end."

How can Rosie speed up at the end of a two-mile run, throught Beth, and felt breathless with the thought of it.

Beth walked to the side of the field, watching Coach. He was round and bald and wore green sweats that hung from his potbelly. He had a whistle around his neck, and as he blew it, Beth saw Ted running out from the locker rooms under the stadium. She waved, but he didn't respond. She had a second of confusion, wondering why he ignored her, and then realized that he was concentrating so hard on lengthening his stride, he hadn't even seen her.

Rosie stood up and bent from the waist, doing cross-overs. Ted, looking lean and blond, was pressing against the bleacher wall, stretching his long legs. The rest of the team, in green sweat suits, warmed up their muscles in various exercises. Then Rosie adjusted her headband and began jogging on the cinder track, her knees as high as her waist.

Should I go over to Ted, Beth wondered, but before she could decide, he came over to the starting line where she stood. "Am I ever glad you're here," he said, bending over her until Beth wondered if he was going to kiss her. Feeling nervous and distracted, she stepped back from him.

"This is going to be a good workout," said Ted, appearing not to notice that Beth had moved. "The Elk Peninsula team was our toughest competition last year."

"Did any of them go to State?" asked Beth, holding her pencil onto the paper, trying to control the jiggles that pulsed through her fingers.

"The tall thin girl over there, Elise, in the brown stripes," Ted said. "She came third in the Double A competition."

"Was that the same race where Rosie came second?"

Ted nodded. "Rosie and Elise have competed against each other since they were freshmen, but Elise has grown a lot taller and I don't think Rosie has much hope of beating her this year. Rosie's too darn short."

The sun beat down on the grassy field. When Ted left to finish his warm-ups, Beth climbed into the bleachers. Three rows were filled with ninth and tenth graders. Lisa and Kit saw Beth and waved. Rosie's parents, Susie, and another of Rosie's sisters waved to Beth as well. Beth waved back and it felt very comfortable knowing that there were people in the stadium who actually knew who she was.

A little while later, Mr. Sealley dashed in. He sat beside Beth and said, "Have I missed anything? I couldn't get away sooner."

"First race is just about to begin," said Beth, happy that he chose to sit with her.

Rosie lined up. She looked like a half-pint next to Elise, from Elk Peninsula. There were eight girls on the cinder track, and as soon as the gun went off, they started like a shot. Rosie and Elise immediately pulled ahead of the others and headed around the field.

Elise started to pull away from Rosie. Elise had a long, steady stride, with her elbows bent loosely at her waist, whereas Rosie moved her arms forward, as if they were part of the energy pulling her along.

Go, Rosie, Beth said under her breath. She was concentrating so much on Rosie that she nearly fell off her seat when Ted said "Hi" right above her head.

"Hi," Beth said, and then her mind went blank.

"Hi, Dad," Ted said as he sat down beside Beth. She felt elated with his sitting there, but didn't know what to say until he started pulling the spikes for his track shoes out of his tote bag.

"Mediums," she said.

"Right on," Ted, said, grinning at her.

Beth looked at his track shoes. They, also, had an "R" on the right foot. She pointed to it and looked at Ted questioningly.

Ted tucked his chin down to his chest. "Coach says I should start on my right foot . . ."

Beth laughed.

"And I can't never remember which one it is." Ted shaded his eyes with his hands, and then peeked out at Beth with a dopey expression on his face.

"I understand," Beth said, going along with the joke. "You can't be perfect at everything."

Rosie and Elise continued to pull ahead of the other runners.

"They lapped them," Ted said after Rosie and Elise had circled the field six times. He squeezed Beth's hand, then let go and stood up.

"What do you mean?" asked Beth, wishing he could stay, but understanding that he had to warm up for his own race.

"It means they're one whole lap ahead of everyone else," he replied, then turned to the stadium stairs.

"Good luck, son," called his dad.

Ted gave them the thumbs-up sign and jogged down to the field.

Shortly after Ted left, Phillip Predo sat down behind Beth and Mr. Sealley.

"Seen Emily?" he asked.

"She's gone into Seattle," said Mr. Sealley.

"Oh," said Phillip. He removed his black beret and

twirled it around and around his fingers, until Beth thought she'd go crazy.

Beth forced herself to concentrate on Rosie. Occasionally, when her eyes just happened to stray to Ted's white-blond hair shining in the sun, and his long, muscled legs in green track shorts, she wondered if she was seeing a mythical prince.

Rosie's family cheered loudly from the midsection of the bleachers, and the rest of the spectators joined in as soon as Rosie and Elise came around for the home stretch. The scorekeeper fired a blank gun.

"That's to indicate the beginning of the last lap," explained Mr. Sealley. "And watch closely, or you'll never believe your eyes."

As if she had received a shot of adrenaline, Rosie's legs began to spin. She pulled ahead. She passed Elise and kept going, her red hair like a fire ball speeding down the track. Elise's body twisted with the effort of keeping up.

All the contestants on the field seemed frozen like statues as they stopped warming up in order to watch. The bleachers bounced with the sound of cheering.

Rosie whirred past. She crossed the finish line a yard ahead of Elise. The bleachers went wild. Rosie pulled off her sweatband and swung it in the air while she jogged slower and slower and finally unwound enough to stand still.

"Unofficial time," the scorekeeper called through the loudspeaker, "eleven-forty-oh-three."

"She beat last year's record," Mr. Sealley said.

Beth took notes, but even though she had seen it with her own eyes, it was hard to believe that her friend Rosie was such a demon on the track.

The boys' hurdles were next. Followed by the girls' hurdles, the girls' hundred-meter dash, the high jump, the broad jump, and the sixteen-hundred-meter run, but no one was nearly as spectacular as Rosie.

Then Ted lined up for the four-hundred-meter dash. Beth clutched her pencil in one hand, her paper in the other, as nervous as if she were running the race. The rows of girls started thumping their feet, shouting, "Go Ted! Go Ted! Go Ted!"

The gun banged. Ted started with his right foot and then it seemed like he spun down the track like lightning, his white hair tumbling over his ears, and his body cutting the finish line string before anyone took a breath.

Mr. Sealley cupped his hands to his mouth and shouted, "Way to go, son! Way to go!"

"He's hot!" exclaimed Phillip Predo behind Beth's head.

Ted scanned the bleachers. The girls went wild. Ted tossed his hair out of his eyes, and seemed to look at each person in turn until finally his gaze rested on Beth, and he winked.

Chapter Twenty-one

Ted jogged to the ticket booth, and Beth ran alongside, panting to keep up. "We'll just make the five-fifteen," Ted said, urging Beth on.

Beth had a moment's worry, whether to pay her own fare or not, but Ted had commuter tickets, and before she knew it, they were racing down the gangplank to the ferry.

The boat was a four-hundred-foot car ferry with a sundeck on top, and seats and a cafeteria filling the huge inside area. Eggie was sitting at one of the tables, his briefcase open in front of him.

"Hi," Eggie said as Beth and Ted slipped into the seats across the table from him. It seemed to Beth that Eggie thought it was perfectly natural that she and Ted were together on the ferry, but to her, it was sort of a marvelous miracle—something she'd wanted to happen ever since she first saw Ted sitting in back row in Algebra, on her first day at Cedar Island High.

"Where are you off to?" Ted asked Eggie.

Eggie shut his briefcase. "I'm going to a *go* match in the International District."

"Do not pass Go," Ted joked, borrowing a line from Monopoly.

"Go?" asked Beth. "What's that?"

"It's an ancient Oriental game," Eggie said, adjusting his glasses on his nose.

"Like chess?"

"More like an elaborate and complicated game of Othello," Eggie said. "A million times more difficult."

"You lost me," Ted said.

"Hmm," Beth said. "I wonder if Frank knows about it. He loves complicated games."

"Hey," Eggie said. "I want to meet your brother."

"He's coming out for Easter," Beth said. "You'll have to drop by our house."

"She lives in Kawaguchi's old place," Ted said, and Beth wondered when, if ever, the house they lived in would be called the Hamilton place.

"What are you guys up to?" Eggie asked as the ferry neared Seattle.

"We're going into Seattle for dinner," Ted said.

"I'll tell you a good place," Eggie said. "It's Mai Chew's in the International District."

"We're going for Mexican Food," said Ted, "But we'll try Mai Chew's another time." He looked at Beth. "Okay?"

She nodded, pleased that there would be another time.

"After I get back from Hawaii. Promise?"

"Promise," Beth said, and grinned because one thing she got top marks in was keeping a promise.

After the ferry had docked, they waved good-bye to Eggie and walked down the waterfront, past the Aquarium, past the park, past the Import Store.

"This way," Ted said, guiding Beth with a hand on her back. The intimacy of his gesture sent warm waves through her and Beth unconsciously slipped an arm around Ted's slim waist.

They crossed the railway tracks, then headed up the long stairs leading up to the Market.

"Race you to the top," Ted said.

Beth craned her head back to look at the building hanging from the edge almost above her.

"Come on," Ted urged.

"Aren't you tired from running all day?" Beth raised her eyebrows until she felt like they disappeared under her bangs.

Ted shook his head.

About two-thirds of the way up the hill, Beth saw several tin umbrellas with CERVEZA written on them, and a pink elephant piñata hanging from a pole. ''I'll race you to the restaurant,'' she said, pointing.

''I'll give you a handicap,'' said Ted. ''I'll race to the top and join you at the restaurant. First one to get there buys dinner.''

Beth took a dollar out of her pocket and waved it in the air. ''We won't each much!'' she said, then bit her tongue, wishing she'd remembered to bring more so she could offer to pay for her own meal.

''Oh, dear,'' Ted said good-humoredly. ''We'd better not work up an appetite.''

Beth crouched to a starting position and, grinning up at him, said, ''On your mark, get set, go!'' They took off up the concrete stairs, two at a time.

In a flash, Ted reached the top, turned to the restaurant, and was sitting underneath one of the tin umbrellas when Beth finally joined him.

''You are out of shape,'' Ted said in a concerned voice.

''Don't I know it,'' Beth said, hanging her head over her knees, trying to catch her breath.

''Too much sitting and not enough exercise,'' Ted said.

Beth nodded, still gasping for air.

''I'm going to have to take you in hand,'' he said, and Beth couldn't agree more, especially when he reached for her hand and led her into the little restaurant.

They lined up, cafeteria-style, along the right side of the room. All along the left side, windows looked out onto the waterfront and the Sound.

Across the Sound, Cedar Island lay like a dark green bubble. In that second, when Beth looked at the island eight miles away, and at the magnificent Olympic Mountains beyond the island, she knew that she would never want to live anywhere else.

''Over here,'' Ted said after they had put their dinner on their trays. He sat down at the farthest table next to the window.

Beth could barely concentrate on eating her dinner because

the little Mexican restaurant with its festive tables and chairs and crepe-paper piñatas seemed magical. The stunning view outside accentuated this image.

Beth took the top off a small basket filled with hand-patted tortillas. She handed one to Ted and put one on her own plate. For some weird fraction of a second she felt like they had eaten Mexican food together before. Then she blinked her eyes, and the feeling of déjà vu left.

Ted talked a little about his mother, and Beth talked a little about Frank, and often they were silent, but even in the silence it seemed they were communicating in a special way.

"No more!" Beth held her hands flat over her plate as Ted offered to go for seconds.

"You're kidding?" Ted said incredulously.

"I'm not!" She patted her stomach.

"I'm still starving," he said. Grinning at her until his dimple deepened, he returned to the food counter and ordered another complete dinner.

Beth felt her jaw drop, until she remembered how Frank used to eat and eat and eat, and he didn't run all the time like Ted did, so it was a wonder that Ted didn't eat even more.

"Do you have a watch?" Ted asked when the sky darkened and they watched the stars twinkle.

Beth shook her head.

"We must be two of a kind," Ted said as he got up to ask the woman behind the counter what time it was.

When he returned to the table, Beth saw the yellow lights of the ferry approaching the Seattle dock.

"We'll have to run to catch the boat if we don't leave right now," said Ted, swallowing the last of his lemonade.

"No more running for me," Beth said. "I'd rather miss the ferry." Then she felt her cheeks redden.

"Me, too," said Ted, and he took her hand and squeezed it as they walked out of the magical restaurant and down the long steps to the waterfront.

The ferry home was crowded. Beth saw Mrs. Atkinson with her husband. As they passed, Mrs. Atkinson said, "How was the track meet?"

While Ted told Mrs. Atkinson the specifics, Beth thought

about her paper for the writing contest. I'll finish it tomorrow, she decided as they left the Atkinsons and found empty chairs near the front of the ferry.

Ted reached for her hand. He laced his fingers in and out of her own, and Beth felt, and loved, the strength of his fingers. It was almost as if she could feel the strength of his whole character in the pressure of his fingers.

"Boo," said a female voice behind them. Beth would have hit the ceiling if Ted hadn't been holding her hand.

"Sorry," said the voice. Beth turned around to face Emily, who swept her manicured fingers through her hair, obviously embarrassed at frightening Beth.

"Hi, Cuz!" Ted frowned in a joking way. "Are you scaring my girl?"

My girl? Did I hear right? thought Beth.

Emily seemed to think nothing of it. She crossed in front of them and sat down on the opposite seat. She was wearing black leather ankle boots, a black leather mini-skirt, and a black, mauve, and white striped blouse with a boat neckline and three-quarter dolman sleeves.

"You look stunning," Beth said.

"Smashing," Ted agreed, squeezing Beth's hand.

"Fantastic," said a male voice behind them.

Beth and Ted swiveled their heads together, and in that instant when their eyes caught, Beth felt a moment of intense joy. Ted was the boy for her. She also knew that he had meant it when he said, "my girl." Her shoulders relaxed and it seemed like they sent a message all the way down her spine. She didn't have to bear up, or hold herself stiff any longer. She could relax and enjoy life for the first time in months.

Phillip Predo swooped off his black beret and bowed toward Emily. She giggled. Phillip pranced around and sat on the seat beside her, twirling his beret around like a Frisbee. Quick as a wink Emily caught the beret and flipped it onto her head. It looked great tucked into the middle of her mass of frizzy blond hair.

Phillip pursed his lips, kissed his fingers in an elaborate gesture, and brushed the kiss in Emily's direction.

"They deserve each other," Ted said quietly in Beth's ear.

And so do we, thought Beth, and realized by saying that, that she no longer ''looked up'' to Ted, and no longer thought of herself as unworthy of his attention.

''Anybody seen Eggie?'' Beth asked and the words weren't out of her mouth a minute before, lo and behold, he walked up to them, balancing his briefcase on his shoulder.

''Hey, Eggie, how'd *go* go?'' Ted asked.

''Gotta go,'' joked Phillip.

''All systems go,'' Eggie said. As he sat down, he imitated the sound of a rocket taking off, causing everyone to burst into laughter.

Too soon the ferry docked. Beth and Ted walked slowly to the Plymouth and Beth slid all the way over to Ted's side when she climbed in. She loved the fact that he didn't have bucket seats, especially when he pulled into her driveway and circled the arbutus tree. He stopped the car, and put his arms around her.

''I had a wonderful . . .'' Beth said softly, but she couldn't finish her sentence because Ted's lips were on her own.

Chapter Twenty-two

Early Sunday morning Beth woke up and immediately reached for her dream book, which she had tucked under her pillow. She had dreamed she was riding an old-fashioned painted horse at a merry-go-round. She could still hear the tinny music in her ears. She grinned to herself, and slipping her feet into her down booties, then retrieving the big hairy monster paper from her desk drawer, began to rework her sentences until everything made sense.

"Breakfast!" Dad called up into her loft. When Beth climbed down the ladder she saw waffles and maple syrup on the table.

"Have fun yesterday?" Mom asked, sitting down at the table in her light gray suit with the moss-green silk blouse.

"Yes." Beth smiled but she couldn't talk. There was so much, and so little to say at the same time.

After breakfast, Beth returned to her paper instead of going to church. She heard the phone ring just as she dotted the last period on the last page.

"Hi. Good morning. How are you?" Ted's deep friendly voice came over the wires.

"Fine. Good. Great," Beth said with a chuckle.

"Doing anything?" Ted asked.

"Nope. I'm all done," Beth said truthfully. "How 'bout you?"

"I had to get up early and wind mandrels for Dad."

"Are you finished?"

"No way. I'm just taking a cocoa break. Emily's here stirring up a storm."

Even though she knew she was being silly, Beth felt the old familiar pangs of jealousy. She blurted out, "How come Emily's always at your place?"

"She lives next door," Ted said. "You probably didn't see her house because it's hidden on the other side of a grove of trees, but she got in the habit of popping by here when Mom was ill, and taking care of her when she could. Now she's got the craziest notion that she needs to take care of Margot, Dad, and me."

"And they don't deserve it." Emily's voice came through the line.

"Oh, yes, they do," Beth said, wishing she could be there to stir cocoa, although she wasn't so sure she wanted to do dishes.

"Don't mind her," Ted's familiar voice returned. "Emily thinks just because she makes cocoa for us, she can also boss us, but it ain't true."

"He's got bad English on top of everything else." It was Emily's voice again and Beth was beginning to feel that there was a three-way conversation going, except her side of it wasn't saying much.

"Emily, go stir the cocoa so Beth and I can talk," Ted said. Then there were no more interruptions and they found plenty to say until Ted had to return to his dad's workshop.

"See you tomorrow," Ted said.

"In Algebra."

"I can pick you up in the morning," he said, "if you don't mind leaving a little early."

"Anything's better than the school bus," Beth responded, then bit her lip for a second before she blurted out, "That's not what I meant at all!"

"I know what you meant," Ted said gently. "I have trouble with words, too."

"You bet he does," Emily interrupted, and, as usual, she had the last word.

• • •

Beth was waiting on the porch when Ted drove up in the Plymouth on Monday morning. He kissed her as soon as she slid into the front seat. He smelled of mint and Irish Spring, and his hair was parted and combed. Beth was wearing loose khaki pants, and a matching blouse that Mom had bought for her. She had tied Mom's teal scarf around her neck and pinned her hair back on one side.

"So my girl's getting glamorous." Ted grinned as he headed down the driveway.

"Taking a few pointers from Emily," Beth said.

"Tell her," Ted said. "She really gets down on herself and doesn't see herself clearly at all."

"Big old hairy monster," muttered Beth. When Ted raised a questioning eyebrow, she told him the jist of her paper for the writing contest, and how she had learned that the negative things she was saying about herself came from a place which wasn't accepting the fact that it was okay to feel frightened and stupid and scared . . .

"Especially since you had to come into a new school, and come in halfway through the school year," Ted added.

"And especially since I repressed the part of me that felt that way," said Beth, "so it got totally out of hand, and took the shape of a monster."

"When you are really a very nice, sensitive, loving person," Ted said warmly.

And Beth grinned, and felt no need to change his mind.

When Ted parked the car and they were walking up to school, he said, "Talk to Emily. She needs to hear some of what you've been telling me. She's always putting herself down."

"I promise," Beth said.

Time seemed to compress and expand. The time with Ted seemed short, but the time away from him seemed endless.

"You're in love," Rosie said at lunch on Thursday, the day before Ted was leaving for Hawaii and Frank was arriving from Boston.

"Can you tell?" Beth rubbed her hand across her face as if trying to rub something off.

"It's in your eyes."

And my heart, thought Beth.

"Is he taking you to the May Day Dance?"

"Oh, rats!" Beth said. "I bet he's forgotten all about it."

"How could he forget? Honestly, I think he'd lose his head if it weren't screwed on so tight. Isn't he planning it through the ASB?"

"He set up the committees and they're doing all the work."

"Delegate. That's Ted's motto."

Beth sighed and wondered privately if she dared mention the dance, even though it seemed fairly obvious that he wasn't planning on inviting anyone else.

"Knowing him, he's probably forgotten," Rosie said. "I wouldn't worry about it. I mean, what more can you expect from a man who can't remember his right foot from his left."

Beth laughed. She finished her sandwich and then said, "You amazed me on Saturday, Rosie. I knew you could run, but I didn't know you could"—and her voice took on emphasis—"Fly! Coach must be so proud of you."

"Oh, Coach makes me so mad," Rosie said, crunching her Milky Way wrapper into a ball, then smashing it into her hand. "I don't know why I bother talking to him. He's such a jerk."

Beth laughed. Rosie had such a wonderful way of getting out her angry feelings. She knew Rosie loved Coach. "What happened?"

"He told me I have to try out for the Georgia Racing Camp," Rosie said indignantly. "Me! I'm a pip-squeak. Much too short. I could never make the Racing Camp." She lowered her eyes and stared at the table.

Beth reached over and grasped Rosie's fist that she was pounding on the table. "Who's inside you, talking like that?" she asked firmly. "Rosie, you know what a good runner you are. How can you give up without even trying?"

"Okay, friend, I'll do it." Rosie popped her head up and smiled. "Why not? Jens will be in Alaska all summer, so I might as well do something. Might as well find out how bad I am."

"Or find out how much more you need to improve," Beth

said. "Don't think about how bad or good you are, just get out there and run."

"Blah," Rosie muttered. "The track team ought to hire you."

"It's as if we all have lots of sides to us, and if we aren't nice to some of our bad sides, they pound their way to the front of us, and sometimes take over."

"Blah," Rosie repeated. "Now you're sounding like Dad when he's wearing his psychiatrist hat."

"So you already know what I'm trying to say."

Rosie was quiet for many minutes, which was so unusual that Beth wondered if she'd come on too strong.

"I will do it," Rosie said in a calmer voice. "I'll try out for the Georgia Racing Camp and I'll do it, not 'cause Coach or you or anybody says to, but because I know, deep inside me, that that's what I want to do."

"Great!" And at that moment, Beth wanted to hug Rosie, her first and best friend at Cedar Island High, and so she did.

Beth caught the school bus home, but Ted stopped by after track practice, kissing her briefly while on the back porch.

"I forgot to tell you," Ted said, pulling away. "I'm not going to school tomorrow. We're leaving on the plane at noon for Hawaii."

He looked so woebegone his dimple almost disappeared. Beth stroked his cheek. "I'll be here when you get back."

"And we'll go to the May Day Dance, okay?"

"You bet," Beth said softly, her voice betraying her excitement.

"And you'll wear your mom's poodle skirt?"

"You remembered?" Beth's voice rose.

"I meant to ask you then," Ted said. "But I got distracted."

"I was going to remind you," said Beth truthfully. "If you didn't get around to asking me."

"You can remind me about anything at any time," Ted said, and he kissed Beth on the forehead, and then again on her lips.

School on Friday seemed strange without Ted. Algebra

was a big bore, topped by the fact that Mr. Ives gave them scads of equations to work out over the vacation.

Beth rode the school bus home, and waited impatiently for Frank until he arrived with Dad on the five-fifteen ferry. Then it felt like old times, even though they were living in Kawaguchi's crazy-mixed-up house.

Chapter Twenty-three

Frank had a short, ruddy-brown beard outlining his long narrow jaw. He had short hair, and a vertical crease between his eyebrows apparently from so much studying. He was exhausted and slept almost all of Saturday in the study.

Mom practiced with the Fifties Dance Band on Saturday afternoon, and Beth went over to Rosie's house. When they got home, Frank was awake, and they would have talked all night, except Dad said, "If we don't get some shut-eye, we'll never get up for church. It's Palm Sunday and Mom's singing a solo."

On Monday the telephone rang, and when Beth answered, Emily said, "How about sailing tomorrow?"

Thinking about Frank, Beth hesitated, wishing she had the nerve to ask Emily if he could come, too.

"Of course it might rain," Emily said, filling in the silence. "But if it doesn't, Dad said we'd be taking the boat out for sure and you're welcome to come."

"My brother's here from back East," Beth blurted out a little too quickly. "He's on a break from graduate work at MIT . . ."

"Is he the brother that Eggie's been wanting to meet?" Emily asked.

"Yes," Beth said, and again the fact that everyone knew everything about everyone on Cedar Island was confirmed.

"Bring him," Emily said. "I'll ask Eggie, too. Then he and your brother can talk while you and I compare notes about the writing contest. Did you hand in your story yet?"

"Yes, I did," Beth said, but felt uneasy and not at all ready to talk about her story with a first-class writer like Emily.

Tuesday, the sky poured buckets. Emily called to postpone the sail until Wednesday. "Eggie's coming," she said. "And Dad was wondering if your parents would like to come, too."

"Is there enough room for all of us?" Beth asked.

"Sure," Emily said. "Thirty-nine feet of boat holds a lot of people, at least for a day's sail."

On Wednesday, the clouds melted, the sun shined, the wind blew across the Sound and the Summers' thirty-nine-foot ketch *Flyboy* sailed on the bay between Cedar Island and Seattle.

Dad took the day off work and he and Mom had a great time helping Emily's parents sail the boat. On the bow, Frank and Eggie talked about math. Emily and Beth joked back and forth, and then Emily taught Beth how to put hot dogs on the alcohol stove in the galley. Thankfully, Emily never mentioned the writing contest.

It was a glorious day with the snowy mountains visible on all sides, and the water sparkling in the sunshine. Grinning to herself, Beth kept looking up at Frank relaxing on the front of the boat. If it hadn't been for Frank's pressuring me to sign up for things, I might never have met Emily, or sailed in their boat, or met Ted, she thought. Several times throughout the day, she wished Ted were returning from Hawaii in time to meet Frank.

"I'm so glad you came home," Beth said as she and Frank walked up the hill to the car. The sailboat had been tied at the dock, and everyone had said their thank-yous and good-byes.

Home. It had such a nice sound. When they drove up the long driveway and saw the late sun casting shadows over their many-sided magical house, Beth was even more convinced that Cedar Island was her home. Even if they did live in a place that people still called the Kawaguchi house.

• • •

"Oh, I'm glad to be home!" It was Ted on the telephone, late Monday night. It had been the first day back at school since Easter. Frank had gone, but Ted was back! "I can hardly wait to see you," he said.

"Did you have fun?" Beth felt her body tingle with delight.

"Caught a few waves," Ted said. "Lost a few others."

"Surfing?"

"You bet."

"Cedar Island's track star hits the boards!" Beth exclaimed.

"I tell ya, if I weren't in such good shape, I'd have lost my board for certain."

Beth couldn't believe they were talking non-stop, and it was ten o'clock at night. She told him all about Easter, all about eating a licorice rabbit, and he told her all about palm trees, big waves, and tropical fish.

Finally Ted said, "I hope I didn't call too late."

"You can call me anytime," Beth replied.

"I'd rather see you," Ted said. "How does tomorrow sound?"

"Great!" Beth could hardly wait.

"I'll pick you up."

"Come early." Beth wondered if she'd even sleep.

"And you be ready."

"I will."

Early the next morning, Beth dressed in a cranberry, cotton-pleated skirt, with a striped crew neck top. Mom and Dad had given her the outfit as an Easter present. Frank had given her a plastic button with the words: "I'm the best ME there is." Beth was attaching the pin to her shirt when she heard tinny music at the back door.

It was Ted playing a ukulele on the porch.

"You're serenading me!" Beth exclaimed as she burst out the door.

"A Hawaiian love song," Ted said. Then he seemed to see her for the first time, and his incredible green eyes widened.

"Look at my girl," he said. "I go away for a week and she does a number on me when I come back."

"Would you rather I wore my snowflake sweater with the fuzz balls?" asked Beth. "And my faded old jeans?"

"No way," Ted said. "I like the new you."

But the truth was, it wasn't the new Beth. It was the same old Beth, only not afraid to let the world see her as she truly was.

Chapter Twenty-four

It seemed like months ago, instead of weeks, that the ASB had planned the May Day Dance. Beth had ironed the poodle skirt and whitened a pair of saddle shoes she had bought at the Goodwill. After hunting through Vintage Clothes in Pioneer Square in the city, she found exactly what she needed to complete her fifties outfit: a white V-neck sweater with a huge blue felt megaphone on the front.

On Friday Beth joined Emily, Kit, Lisa, Phillip, and Ray in the cafeteria to decorate for the dance that evening. Coach halted track practice an hour early, and Rosie and Ted ran in to help. Rosie blew up balloons until she was red in the face.

"Stop," said Beth. "You've run out of air."

"Never," Emily said. "Rosie can talk solid for three days and not run out of air."

"*Blllt.*" Rosie, blowing a rasberry at Emily.

"You're in a good mood," Beth said.

"I don't know why," Rosie said. "Jens leaves tomorrow for six months in Alaska."

"Maybe you're feeling like you want to cut loose?" Emily suggested.

"No," Rosie said slowly. "I love him, but I am feeling like it's a good thing to have some space. I've got my whole life ahead of me and it seems kind of silly to get too serious too soon."

"Right!" Emily said, dramatically crashing her fist through the air.

Phillip drew cartoons of fifties characters on life-size sheets of white butcher paper, and hung them from the walls. While Ray Nishimoto and Ted strung crepe paper with the help of two twelve-foot ladders, Kit and Lisa set up tables. Beth and Emily helped Rosie with the rest of the balloons, and then they climbed the ladders and tossed them into the crepe paper net above the dance floor.

When Mr. Bellga arrived with Eggie to set up the speakers and microphones for the band, Eggie introduced him to Beth. His dad said, "Your mom has a lovely voice. She could have been a professional singer."

"Thank you," said Beth, although her response seemed inadequate. Beth got thinking about words again, and about the paper she had handed in for the writing contest. She'd been so busy she had forgotten to worry about whether she would win or lose the contest, but the outcome didn't really matter. I did my best, she thought, and those words took on a special meaning. It was as if she finally *knew* what they meant.

By five-thirty, the cafeteria looked more fifties than The Dew Drop Inn. Ted had barely spoken to Beth because he was so busy making sure all the details were taken care of. When most of the work had been completed, he said, "Can you get a ride home with Eggie? He lives near you."

"Sure," Beth said, trying not to be disappointed.

Ted flicked his fingers at her in a quick salute. "See you on the dot of eight," he said.

"I'll be ready."

When Beth entered the kitchen, she greeted Mom, who had just put dinner in the oven. She was rubbing her palms together, and Beth said, "Are you nervous about singing tonight or something?"

"No," Mom said shortly.

"You're never nervous in church," Beth said.

Mom wagged her head back and forth.

"Tell me what's going on!" Beth insisted.

"I'm nervous."

"Why?"

" 'Cause I haven't sung in front of a high school crowd for twenty-five years."

"Go on."

"And what if they boo me off the stage?"

"So what?"

"I'll embarrass you."

"Not me," Beth said, and she then hugged Mom. "I'm not embarrassed by your taking a risk like this. I'll be embarrassed if you hide in your garden all the time and refuse to find out whether you're a success or not."

"How did you learn so much?" Mom asked, straightening her shoulders. Beth could tell Mom felt better.

"I had good teachers," Beth said, then kissed Mom on the cheek before going into the bathroom to soak in the tub.

After her bath, Beth blew her hair dry, brushing it off her face in soft waves. She ate a small dinner, sitting at the teak table in her cosy dressing gown. Dad fussed and seemed more nervous than Mom had been earlier.

"Relax," Beth said.

"I can't help it," Dad said. "My beautiful daughter's first big dance, and my beautiful wife's debut as a soloist with the Fifties Dance Band."

"We'll be all right," Mom said calmly. When Beth looked at her in surprise, Mom gave her the thumbs-up sign.

Dad drove Mom to Mr. Bellga's, leaving Beth alone in the house to put on the poodle skirt, the cheerleader's V-neck sweater over a white cotton blouse, and the floppy saddle shoes. I wonder if I'll be able to dance in these, thought Beth as she stuffed tissues into the toes to take up space.

When Dad returned to the house, Beth was standing in the middle of the kitchen as if rooted to the spot.

"What's the matter?" Dad asked, giving her a hug.

"I'm scared."

"What about?"

"I don't know."

"Are they announcing the writing contest winners tonight?"

"Yes, but I don't care about that."

"It doesn't matter to me either, whether you win or not," Dad said. "I'll always love you."

"I know," Beth said, and she returned Dad's hug, and felt better.

Ted arrived ten minutes early. He wore a black worsted suit with long, thin lapels and deep cuffs. He had a white silk scarf tucked around his neck.

"This is my dad's wedding suit," he said, looking a little foolish.

"It looks great!" exclaimed Beth, and wished she had the nerve to hug Ted in front of Dad. Ted looked like he needed one.

Ted handed Beth a small gold box.

"A gardenia!" As she opened the box, the strong odor permeated the room. "I love it," Beth said and her eyes met Ted's.

"Oh, my goodness," Dad said, blinking his eyes. "That reminds me of my first date. A girl named . . ." He paused and grinned suddenly at them. "Nora."

"That's my mom," Beth said with a grin.

Ted took the fragile white flower out of the box and pinned it to the shoulder of her V-neck sweater.

"It's perfect," Beth said, taking a deep sniff.

"Just like you," Ted said.

Beth shook her head. "Not me."

"You're perfect just the way you are," insisted Ted.

"Even without my mask?"

"Especially without your mask."

Ted bent over her, but Beth grinned and stepped back because she didn't want him to kiss her in front of Dad.

"I'll see you in a little while," Dad said as Ted and Beth got into the Plymouth. "I'm coming up to chaperon."

Dad's really coming to see Mom and me at our first big event on Cedar Island, thought Beth, and it seemed perfectly logical that he would want to do so.

The cafeteria was transformed. The band played non-stop, and Nora Hamilton was a big hit. Beth finally took off her saddle shoes and danced in her white bobby socks.

"Your mom's terrific," Emily said as she swirled by with Phillip Predo. Beth thought so, too.

Mom sang "Wayward Wind," "Mr. Sandman," and "The Tennessee Waltz." When she started singing "Why Do Fools Fall in Love," Beth looked up at Ted, and he looked down at her, and their eyes locked. They rocked together in the middle of the floor, forgetting to dance.

Jens and Rosie hung onto each other as they slowly circled the dance floor. Jens was wearing zoot-suiter pants and a black dinner jacket with a red carnation in the lapel. Rosie wore a green silk dress with ruffles down the front and a tight belt around her waist.

"You look adorable," Beth said when she and Ted waltzed back.

"You like it better than my sweats?" Rosie swung her ponytail when Beth nodded agreement.

Mom sang a song from the Teddy Bears: "To Know Him Is to Love Him." At that moment Beth saw Brendon Bart dancing with Lisa. Brendon wore a moth-eaten coon-skin coat that made him look even more like a teddy bear than before.

The band took a break, and while Ted hustled up some refreshments, Beth joined Dad. He was talking to Mrs. Atkinson, her English Lit teacher.

"We've judged the entries in the writing contest," Mrs. Atkinson said, smiling at Beth.

Beth held her breath and then, realizing what she was doing, relaxed, and said to herself, So what? I did my best.

"We plan to announce the winners during the next intermission," Mrs. Atkinson continued.

Winners? Beth pushed the thought out of her mind when Ted appeared with lemonade and brownies. Soon the music started again.

"Your mom's going over big," breathed Emily into Beth's ear as they brushed past each other on the dance floor.

"I'm glad," Beth said.

"Can I cut in?" Phillip tapped Ted on the shoulder, and Beth was transferred to Phillip's stiff arms.

"Relax," she said. "Loosen up."

"I get all sweaty when I have to be out in public like this," complained Phillip.

"Why did you come?"

"I didn't want to miss out on a good time."

"How can you have a good time if you can't relax?"

Phillip pulled his beret over his forehead. "I'm relaxed," he said.

"Okay," Beth said.

"Don't bug me," said Phillip. "Or I might draw a cartoon of you for the editorial page."

Beth laughed. "Threats will get you nowhere."

"You've changed," Phillip said. "You used to be scared of your own shadow."

"I suppose you could say that," Beth said, thinking of the monster on the back of the bus.

Mom sang "Young Love," and Ted, thankfully, cut back in. He held Beth so close the gardenia got crushed. The potency of the flower washed over her like warm rain. Beth no longer felt like the black and white bird she had seen trying to hide on the leafless vine during the storm. Now she felt more like an exotic and colorful bird.

During the second intermission, Mrs. Atkinson walked onto the stage. When she spoke into the microphone, there was complete silence.

"I am here to announce the winners of the writing contest," Mrs. Atkinson said in her soft voice. "Eggie informs me that there is a surplus in the ASB Treasury, thanks to the wonderful turnout at this dance."

"And thanks to the fact that the band isn't charging us," Ted whispered in Beth's ear. She was paying so much attention to Mrs. Atkinson that his words practically slipped by her.

"The ASB, in a secret vote, elected to donate their profits to send two delegates to the writing workshop this summer," Mrs. Atkinson said. "Therefore it gives me great pleasure to announce that both the winner of the writing contest, Emily Summers, and first runner-up, Beth Hamilton, will be eligible to attend the Young Author's Workshop at the University of Washington. Congratulations to you both.''

Beth stood stock-still, not believing what she had just heard. Ted patted her on the back. Then he bent over and touched his lips to her forehead. Beth came back to earth, back to the cafeteria-ballroom. She flung her arms around Ted and hugged him.

''You won!'' Rosie said, bouncing over to Beth. ''I knew you would.''

''You mean I'm first runner-up,'' Beth corrected.

''Whatever,'' Rosie said, and she winked. Beth had the distinct feeling that what Rosie had said was true. What she had won was the battle with herself, and she'd won it by making a friend of her own worst enemy: that force inside herself that wanted to put her down.

Emily swung over in her pleated black skirt and blouse. She had a mauve silk flower tucked into her thick frizzy hair. ''Congratulations,'' Emily cried, hugging Beth.

Beth hugged her back and then began giggling out of sheer happiness.

''I'm so glad that you won, too,'' Emily said. ''We'll get to take the course together.''

Beth grinned, and she continued to grin as Eggie, Brendon, Ray, Kit, Lisa, and Phillip huddled around, congratulating them.

''Good work,'' Ted whispered in her ear as they started dancing again.

''It was easy,'' Beth said. ''Almost as easy as speaking.'' And then she smiled to herself, enjoying the feeling of being in Ted's arms, without any need for words.

They moved around the floor, silent. Mom sang an old Elvis song, ''Hound Dog,'' and followed it with several other Elvis songs. Beth and Ted rock and rolled and laughed the whole time with each other. Then Mr. Bellga took the microphone and announced: ''The Bunny Hop.''

The lights brightened. Ted, as ASB President, led the chain. Beth was right behind, and behind her the rest of the school hung on in a long twisting line.

"Forward, back, forward two three," Mr. Bellga chanted as the band played. Soon the room was throbbing with the noise of pounding feet. Ted circled into the middle, and out, and then pulled a streamer hanging from the crepe paper net above them. The net broke. The band played "Now Is the Hour," while everyone jumped for balloons.

"There goes all my air," Rosie said, planting her hands on her hips in disgust.

"There's plenty more where that came from," Jens said, and he pecked Rosie on the lips.

Beth barely noticed. She was too busy looking into Ted's incredible green eyes.

"Time to go, you two," Emily said.

But neither Ted or Beth moved.

"Two of a kind," Emily said, shaking her mass of blond hair.

Beth slipped an arm around Ted's waist and led him to the door. It was the end of the most wonderful night of her life, but she was positive, too, that it was only the beginning of many more.

"Let's do this again sometime," Ted said as they reached the Plymouth.

"Let's," Beth said, and she raised her lips to his.

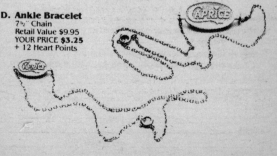

Now that you're reading the best in teen romance, why not make that *Caprice* feeling part of your own special look? Four great gifts to accent that "unique something" in you are all yours when you collect the proof-of-purchase from the back of any current *Caprice* romance!

Each proof-of-purchase is worth 3 Heart Points toward these items available <u>only</u> from *Caprice*. And what better way to make them yours than by reading the romances every teen is talking about! Start collecting today!

Proof-of-purchase is worth 3 Heart Points toward one of four exciting premiums bearing the distinctive *Caprice* logo

CAPRICE PREMIUMS
Berkley Publishing Group, Inc./Dept. LB
200 Madison Avenue, New York, NY 10016

PROOF OF
PURCHASE
—3—
HEART POINTS
♥ ♥ ♥
DETAILS INSIDE